GiRL PoWer

Other fantastic books in the growing Faithgirlz™ library

BIBLES

The NIV Faithgirlz Bibles
The NKJV Faithgirlz Bible
NIV Faithgirlz Backpack Bibles

FICTION

Natalie Grant's Glimmer Girls Series

London Art Chase
(Book One)
A Dolphin Wish
(Book Two)
Miracle in Music City
(Book Three)
Light Up New York
(Book Four)

Samantha Sanderson Series

At the Movies (Book One)
On the Scene (Book Two)
Off the Record (Book Three)
Without a Trace (Book Four)

Good News Shoes Series

Riley Mae and the
Rock Shocker Trek
(Book One)
Riley Mae and the
Ready Eddy Rapids
(Book Two)
Riley Mae and the
Sole Fire Safari
(Book Three)

The Girls of Harbor View

Girl Power (Book One)
Take Charge (Book Two)
Raising Faith (Book Three)
Secret Admirer (Book Four)

Sophie's World Series (2 books in 1)

Meet Sophie
Sophie Steps Up
Sophie and Friends
Sophie's Friendship Fiasco
Sophie Flakes Out
Sophie's Drama

Check out www.faithgirlz.com

faithgirlz

Girls of Harbor View

GiRL PoWeR

including GiRL PoWeR and MySTeRY BuS

Melody Carlson

ZONDERkidz

ZONDERKIDZ

Girl Power
Copyright © 2007, 2012 by Melody Carlson

Mystery Bus
Copyright © 2007, 2012 by Melody Carlson

This title is also available as a Zondervan ebook.
Visit www.zondervan.com/ebooks.

Requests for information should be addressed to:
Zonderkidz, 3900 *Sparks Dr. SE, Grand Rapids, MI 49546*

This edition: ISBN 978-0-310-75361-2

Library of Congress Cataloging-in-Publication Data

Carlson, Melody.
    [Project, girl power]
    Girl power / by Melody Carlson.
        p. cm. — (Girls of Harbor View ; [bk. 1]) (Faithgirlz!)
        Summary: Morgan, Carlie, Amy, and Emily become friends when they join
    together to avoid a bully, and then undertake a project to clean up the shabby
    trailer park where they all live.
    ISBN 978-0-310-73045-3 (softcover)
        [1. Mobile home parks—Fiction. 2. Friendship—Fiction. 3. Bullies—Fiction.
    4. Christian life—Fiction. 5. Oregon—Fiction.] I. Title.
    PZ7.C216637Gir 2012
    [Fic]—dc23   2011051691

Editor: Kim Childress
Cover design: Ron Huizinga

Printed in the United States

16 17 18 19 20 21 22 23 /DCI/ 19 18 17 16 15 14 13 12 11 10 9 8 7 6 5 4 3 2 1

So we fix our eyes not on what is seen, but what is unseen.
For what is seen is temporary, but what is unseen is eternal.

— 2 Corinthians 4:18

chapter one

"Hey you!" boomed a voice from down the street. Morgan's head jerked around just in time to see three boys on bikes, about a block away, but quickly speeding straight toward them.

"Oh, no," groaned Carlie. "It's *them!*"

"Ignore the jerks," Morgan told her new friend. Then she stuck out her chin and continued to walk at the same casual speed. "And slow down, Carlie. You know they're just trying to scare us."

It was the first time the two girls had walked home from school together, and Morgan had hoped it was the beginning of a new friendship.

"Hey, who said you could walk down our street?" hollered that same grating voice. A bike tire skidded to a halt right next to Carlie. On it sat redheaded, freckle-faced Derrick Smith. He always reminded Morgan of an overgrown turnip with a bad butch. Unfortunately, he was the self-appointed leader of this new gang of seventh-grade bullies.

"*Ignore!*" Morgan hissed to Carlie as she continued to walk, humming a tuneless song that was meant to inspire confidence. Then she noticed Carlie's dark eyes grow wider as another boy screeched up, right next to Morgan this time. It was Jeff Sanders, of all people. A third boy Morgan didn't recognize cut off the girls from the front. Morgan glared at Jeff, wondering what he was doing with this crowd. Normally, he seemed like a pretty nice guy. She looked him square in the eye, and to her relief, he glanced away uncomfortably.

"Why don't you guys get a life and leave us alone?" Morgan said in her bravest voice.

"Cuz you're on our turf!" Derrick sneered at her and then thumped Carlie on the shoulder. She jumped away from him, bumping into Morgan. "And we don't like sharing our turf with trailer trash," he said, laughing loudly right in poor Carlie's face.

"Leave her alone!" yelled Morgan. Now Carlie looked scared. Hopefully she wasn't going to fall apart. Morgan wasn't sure that she'd be able to defend both of them.

Then, to Morgan's surprise, Carlie threw back her shoulders, put her hands on her hips, and glared at Derrick. "Back off!" she yelled. Morgan stared at her new friend, certain that flashes of lightning had just shot from Carlie's eyes.

"That's right," said Morgan. "You guys need to just chill."

"And keep your filthy hands off me, or you'll be sorry!" Carlie shook a clenched fist at Derrick.

Morgan admired Carlie's nerve, but she hoped this girl didn't have anything crazy in mind. Two sixth-grade girls against three seventh-grade boys didn't stack up very well. Just then Morgan noticed a man across the street. He was slowly wheeling his trash can out to the curb. He looked even older than her grandma, but the presence of a nearby adult renewed her confidence.

"You don't own this street, Derrick Smith!" She spoke loudly, hoping to draw the attention of the old man. "What's your problem, anyway? We're just minding our own business, and you guys are acting like total jerks." It seemed to be working, because the man by the trash can was peering across the street at them.

She shook her finger at Jeff now. "And I don't get you, Jeff. I mean, you used to be nice to me, and your mom's pretty good friends with my mom. What's up with that?"

"Come on, Derrick," said Jeff in an offhanded way. "I thought you said you had something to show us anyway."

"All right," said Derrick. "*This time*, we'll let you girls off with just a warning. But I don't want to see you on our turf again." Then he peeled out, and the other two boys followed.

Carlie's eyes were still bright with anger. "Those stupid creeps! They act like they own the whole neighborhood. This is the second time this week I've been pestered by them. Who do they think they are, anyway?"

"My mom says they're 'wannabes.'" Morgan kept her voice calm as she started walking again, but she felt sort of wobbly inside, and her knees were a little shaky. Of course, she wouldn't admit she was frightened to Carlie. Not right now anyway. She didn't know the girl that well yet. Besides, Morgan liked for people to think she was brave. It made her feel safer somehow.

"What's a 'wannabe'?" asked Carlie as she paused to readjust her backpack strap.

"Kids who *want to be* like someone else, like these guys 'wannabe' like a gang. Didn't you notice they all had similar kinds of jackets? Kinda like a real gang."

"So what's the difference between 'wannabes' and real gang members? They both dress alike and they both push people around."

"Yeah, maybe there isn't much difference. I don't know for sure."

"It's funny," said Carlie as they continued walking. "My parents moved away from Southern California — before us kids were even born — just to get away from junk like this. Now here we are in this little podunk town in Oregon, and it's the same old, same old."

"So … uh … were you scared, Carlie?"

"Yeah, sure. In fact, I was really scared at first. Then I just got real mad. I imagined my dad hunting down that Derrick kid and teaching him a thing or two. That made me feel a whole lot better. Man, you were really cool, Morgan."

"Well, I was scared too. I just tried not to show it. I wish those guys would get a clue. That's the second run-in I've had with them this week too. I can't imagine putting up with that kind of crud all summer."

"Me neither."

Morgan looked up at the cloudless blue sky. The morning fog had burned off now, and there was hardly a breeze at all. "And this weather could almost make you think that summer's really here."

"I know." Carlie smiled. "I can't believe there are only two weeks of the school year left. I can't wait for summer vacation and hanging out on the beach — all that fun in the sun."

Morgan laughed. "Well, girl, it's plain to see you haven't lived on the Oregon coast during summertime yet. Or else you'd know that summer and nice weather don't always go hand in hand around here. Didn't you guys just move here a couple months ago?"

"Yeah, we came up here from northern California. My dad got laid off from his old job, and my uncle wanted him to come up here and work on his fishing boat. We've been here since the end of March."

"I've been hoping to get to know you," Morgan said, trying to think of why she hadn't reached out to this girl sooner. "But you usually zip off right after school. And I never see you playing outside around the trailer park."

"That's 'cause I usually watch my little brothers after school. But today Mama's at Tia Maria's house, so I get a break."

"Who's Tia Maria?"

"My aunt Maria. *Tia* is Spanish for 'aunt.'"

"Oh, yeah. I don't have any aunts. But I have a grandma. We're living with her right now — until my mom's business takes off better. Our house is at the west side of the park, near the entrance. You can go through our backyard straight over to the dunes, and then the Harbor is only about a ten-minute walk from there."

"Cool. Our house is close to the front too, just a couple of spaces down from you."

"I know. I saw you move into the Porter's old place. I kind of like to keep track of who lives where at the park. I was even thinking about getting a paper route, but you have to be thirteen, and I won't be until July." Morgan stopped and pointed up ahead. "Look, it's those stupid jerks again. It looks like they knocked down that new girl, what's-her-name. We better go help."

They both started running, and Carlie easily kept up. Once again Morgan felt surprised by this girl. Up until today, Morgan had assumed that this girl with the pretty curls and cutsie clothes was too prissy to be a very good friend for her. But today she was seeing a whole different side of her.

When Morgan and Carlie reached where the new girl had been knocked down, Amy Ngo was there too. Amy was helping the downed girl to stand. The girl's jeans were muddy and torn, and her face was streaked with tears. She let Amy help untangle her from her bike then stood and wiped her tears with the back of her hand.

"Thanks," she mumbled, looking down at her bike.

Morgan bent over to pick up the bike, and Carlie knelt to examine the front tire. "It looks like you might have a bent wheel," she said with a frown.

"What happened?" asked Morgan.

"I saw the *whole* thing," exclaimed Amy Ngo importantly. Some of the kids called her Amy "Ngo it All." She'd skipped a grade and was the smartest kid in their class, as well as the teacher's pet. But worst of all she seemed to like for everyone to know it too. Morgan had always kept a safe distance from this girl.

Amy continued her take on the accident as if she were testifying in court. "It was that Derrick Smith. He's the leader of that gang of delinquent boys. Jeff Sanders and Brett Johnson were both with him. But it was primarily Derrick who was harassing Emily. I was about a block behind her and it looked like she was getting away from them, but then the boys were all around her, and the next thing I knew, Derrick poked a stick right into Emily's front tire, and she flipped over into that puddle." Amy paused to catch her breath. "What a mess!"

Morgan looked at Emily now — so that was her name. Leave it to Ngo it All to know that too. The knee where Emily's jeans had torn was bleeding and looked pretty bad. Hopefully it wouldn't need stitches. Morgan had gotten stitches in her foot last summer after she'd stepped on a broken bottle in the sand. Along with a tetanus shot.

"You should probably clean that knee up, Emily," she suggested. It felt strange to use her name since they hadn't officially met ... well ... other than when Miss Thurman introduced her in class. But that shouldn't count since, as usual, Morgan hadn't been paying too close of attention. "I'm Morgan," she continued. "And I live in Harbor View too. You're in my class at Washington."

Emily nodded then tugged at the torn part of her jeans as if to put them back together again. "My favorite jeans," she said a little desperately. "Ruined."

"It's your knee that looks ruined to me," observed Morgan. She wondered about Emily's priorities.

"Oh, no!" Emily cried as she looked all around. "I lost my house key! I must have dropped it when I fell."

So all four girls searched all around the ground, but without any luck.

"It's probably in the bottom of that puddle," suggested Amy, poking around with the stick that Derrick had used to trip up Emily's bike.

"I don't think we're going to find it," said Carlie.

"I can't get into my house," said Emily, who looked once again on the verge of tears.

"Well, you need to take care of that knee right now," said Morgan firmly as she took Emily by the arm. "Come on over to my house, and my grandma can clean it and bandage it for you." She glanced at the other girls. "You guys come too. Carlie, you bring her bike. And you get her backpack, Amy."

The funny thing was that the girls followed Morgan's orders without even questioning what gave her the authority to tell them what to do. And within minutes they were walking into her house.

"Grandma, these are some of my friends," began Morgan as the four girls all piled into her living room. Then she pointed them out, one by one, introducing them to her grandma. "And this is my grandma, Mrs. Evans," she finished.

"Pleasure to meet you, girls."

"And Emily had a wreck on her bike," Morgan continued. "And she lost her key and is locked out of her house. I thought maybe you could look at her knee, Grandma."

"Come on in here, child," said Grandma kindly, just exactly how Morgan knew she would. "Sit yourself right down, and I'll clean up that scrape."

Emily looked uncomfortable as she climbed onto the kitchen stool. Her face was pale and kind of pinched-looking. Morgan wasn't sure if it was from the hurt knee or just the strangeness of everything. To be honest, it was kind of strange for Morgan too. She'd never really had any friends inside her house before, and now suddenly here were three girls she hardly knew that she'd just introduced as "her friends." Was that crazy or what?

Just then Morgan remembered how she'd specifically asked God to send her a friend. It was after a sermon at her church just last week. The pastor had challenged the congregation to ask God for the impossible. At the time, it hadn't seemed even slightly possible that Morgan would ever find one single friend to hang with. Now she had *three*. Or so it seemed.

chapter two

Emily tried not to flinch as Morgan's grandma gently
cleansed the dirt from her knee. More than anything, she
was determined not to cry. She'd already shamed herself
once by crying when those stupid boys knocked her off her
bike. Then to meet these three girls while she was blubbering
like a baby ... It was just like the nightmares she'd had about
moving here. They probably thought she was a real dork.

She studied Mrs. Evans's wrinkled face as she carefully dabbed some ointment on the wound. Emily had
never been this close to a black person before. Suddenly,
she wondered why people called them *blacks*. This woman's
skin was actually light brown, just about the same shade
as a copper penny that had darkened with age. And her
hair was white and soft looking, pulled back away from her
face and knotted into a bun. But it was her eyes that drew
Emily's attention. The color of a Hershey bar, they had a
look of kindness in them. Emily instinctively liked Morgan's grandma, but at the same time she felt cautious too.
Where she came from, blacks and whites didn't mix much.
Her mother had always told her that everyone was "the
same beneath the skin," but her dad had said it wasn't so.

Her dad said a lot of other things that she'd rather forget, but he was far away now. Even so, she felt relieved that he didn't know about Morgan and her grandma, or the other girls for that matter.

"There's some peanut brittle in the pantry, Morgan," Mrs. Evans called over her shoulder as she taped a square of gauze over Emily's wounded knee. Morgan had loaned her a pair of shorts to wear while her knee was being bandaged, but now Emily felt slightly embarrassed as she looked down at her pale, skinny legs.

"Why don't you pour yourself and your friends some milk to go with it?" Mrs. Evans finished securely taping the bandage then smiled at Emily. "There now, sugar. How's that?"

"Good. Thanks a lot, Mrs. Evans."

"Oh, why don't you just call me Grandma," she said. "*Mrs. Evans* sounds so formal to me. When I was a little girl all my friends called my grandmother *Grandma*, and I liked that. You don't mind sharing me, do you, Morgan?"

Morgan shook her head as she poured four glasses of milk. "Fine with me." Emily liked how Morgan's long, narrow braids swung when she moved her head.

"I'll give your trousers a quick rinse-off, Emily," Grandma said as Emily slid off the stool. "Then I'll toss them in the dryer for a few minutes."

"Thanks," Emily whispered as she pushed her long blonde hair behind her ears.

"Here's a place for you," said Morgan, pulling out a chair for Emily. Emily felt even more self-conscious as she joined the other girls at the small dinette table. The three of them quietly munched and sipped their milk, casting quick glances at one another. Emily wondered if it was because of her. Maybe she shouldn't be sticking around.

Suddenly, she felt like an intruder. Maybe these three had been friends for a long time, and maybe they didn't want her to be here with them. She watched Amy delicately nibbling on a small piece of peanut brittle. She didn't know if Amy was Chinese or Japanese or what, but she thought she had the most beautiful skin she'd ever seen. It looked as smooth as a porcelain doll. And her shiny black hair was cut as straight as a knife's edge right across her forehead. The sides were just as even, as if each hair had been carefully measured and cut to perfection.

Across the table from her, Carlie set down her empty milk glass and leaned forward. "We need to do something about this gang," she said in a hushed tone. "Should we tell our parents about them, report them to the authorities, or what?"

No one said anything, and Emily felt certain that *she* didn't want to be the one to tell on them or report them. Mostly, she just wanted to forget the whole stupid thing. But what if Carlie was a tattletale kind of girl? She studied Carlie's neat white blouse with pink flowers embroidered on the collar. It looked as if someone had just ironed it. Her long, thick curls fell over her shoulders, almost like a cape. Yes, thought Emily, she might be the type to tattle.

"No, we don't want to tell," stated Morgan, glancing over to where Grandma had settled back into the living room, intently watching the *Oprah* show on TV. To Emily's relief, Carlie nodded in agreement and Morgan continued. "Tattling will just get them really mad at us. And then they might try and get revenge. We don't need that."

"Maybe not," said Amy, "but it's not fair that we can't walk down the street without being *accosted*." Emily wondered if Amy was trying to impress them with her big vocabulary.

"That's right," said Carlie, "we shouldn't worry about being safe in our own neighborhood. That's just wrong."

"Maybe we should try walking to and from school together," suggested Morgan. "You know what they say, 'There's safety in numbers.'"

"Yeah," said Carlie. "That's a great idea!"

"We could even have some sort of a battle plan," continued Morgan. "I mean, in case the thugs still come after us. We could stand up to them and tell them that we won't take it anymore. We could tell them to go get a life!" She pounded the table for emphasis, and everyone nodded in what appeared to be agreement. Including Emily. She liked this plan for a couple of reasons. For one thing, it would allow her to continue to hang with these girls. Besides that, she realized she'd be walking to school now that her bike was messed up.

"Well, I have to go home now," announced Amy. "But if we're really going to do this thing — I mean, if we're going to walk to school together — I suggest that we meet at 7:45 at the park entrance."

"Ugh," groaned Morgan. "Why do you go to school so early?"

"I happen to *like* being early." Amy frowned at her.

"Man, I never leave before eight," said Morgan.

"And I don't usually walk to school," admitted Carlie. "Tia Maria drops me off on her way to work. But I can walk with you guys if that'd help."

"Yeah," said Morgan. "We need to stick together. Four girls will look a lot stronger than just three." She turned back to Amy. "Okay, how about a compromise? How about if we leave at *five* 'til eight?"

"Seven fifty," said Amy in a stubborn voice. Morgan scowled, but then she agreed. So it seemed to be settled. But then Amy and Carlie said good-bye and left, and suddenly Emily felt even more uncomfortable. Was she supposed to go home now too? She knew she could sit on the little front porch and wait for Mom and Adam to get home. Or maybe she could try to break in through a window ...

"When does your family usually get home?" asked Morgan, as if reading Emily's thoughts.

"It's just my mom and brother," she explained. "And they don't get home until around six, but I could go wait on the porch —"

"No, it's okay. I mean, you can stay here as long as you like. No problem."

"Thanks," said Emily. "Do you think I should put my jeans back on now?"

"Let's go see if they're dry yet," said Morgan, leading her out past the kitchen to a tiny laundry room. Morgan opened the dryer and pulled out the jeans, giving them a shake then handing them to Emily.

"Thanks," said Emily. "And thanks for letting me wear your shorts. They're really cute. They look just like real bandanna handkerchiefs; just like the ones my grandpa used to blow his nose on." She wished she hadn't said that.

Morgan laughed, a rich, deep laugh that was full of warmth. "That's because I made them out of real bandannas. Of course, no one actually blew their nose on them … at least not that I know of."

"That's amazing." Emily looked down at the shorts she was still wearing. "You actually made these yourself? Can you really sew? Like real clothes and everything?"

"Sure. I love to just make things up right out of my head. Usually I draw the design first, and then I cut it out and sew it. Come to my room, and I'll show you my latest."

Emily followed Morgan to a small bedroom just off the kitchen, and Morgan opened her closet, pulling out a colorful dress. "My latest creation," she said proudly.

"Wow! That is really cool! I like this fabric. It looks different."

"It's called batik. They use wax and dye to make these patterns on the cloth. My mom got it for me. It's from Indonesia." Morgan held the unfinished dress up, and Emily could just imagine how it would look on. Morgan was tall and thin, and the dress would be perfect against her golden-brown skin.

"I wish I knew how to sew." Emily looked at her jeans and the torn knee. "Then at least I could fix this stupid hole."

"Hey, let me patch it for you." Morgan snatched the jeans out of her hands and pulled out a brightly colored sewing basket, then she flopped onto her bed, which was really a futon covered with a zebra-print fabric. She pushed her glasses up the bridge of her nose and studied the tear from several angles. "And how 'bout I make your jeans a little more interesting while I'm at it?"

"That'd be great." Emily sank into a furry beanbag chair and looked around Morgan's room. Like Morgan, it was interesting. Really interesting. Lots of beaded necklaces and bracelets hung over her dresser mirror. Interesting pieces of fabric seemed to be draped everywhere. Emily wasn't sure if they were decorations or just sewing projects in process. But Morgan's room felt good to her. And fun.

"I like your room, Morgan."

Morgan nodded without looking up. "Thanks, I like it too. But what I really want to do is paint some murals on the walls. Mom says I shouldn't since this is really Grandma's house, but I don't think Grandma would mind. I want to paint a big tiger coming out of the jungle by the closet and maybe a zebra over there by the door."

Emily tried to imagine it and smiled. "That would be so cool. I wish I could do something like that to my room. It's pretty boring. Just plain white walls and an ugly brown carpet with a stain shaped like Texas in the middle."

"So why don't you paint a mural on your walls?" Morgan bit a thread with her teeth and looked up.

"Oh, I don't know … I'm not that artistic. I wouldn't even know where to —"

"I could help," offered Morgan. She held the jeans up. Emily couldn't believe it. Morgan had already sewn a little piece of fabric — along with a ribbon and matching purple button — right over the tear, and now the jeans looked really cool.

"Morgan, you are totally amazing! That looks really great. Thank you so much. I thought my jeans were ruined, and now they look better than before." She almost admitted that these were the only jeans she'd been able to bring with her on this move. But she didn't. How could she explain to Morgan that they'd left their previous home with only the clothes on their backs? She wasn't about to admit that.

"No problem, Em. I'm glad I could help." Morgan set her sewing basket aside. "Want to listen to some music? I have a new Newsboys CD."

"Sure, I've never heard of them. Are they good?"

"Pretty good. They're a Christian group."

Emily nodded politely like she was interested, but it actually sounded kind of strange.

"Come on over here and you can do the lyrics with me."

Emily sat down on the futon next to Morgan and peered down at the tiny print on the paper. She tried her best to listen to the music and follow along with the fast-paced lyrics. Morgan knew most of the songs by heart. Emily tried to sing along, but it was like her words were in a blender, being chopped and spun until they were senseless. Finally, she messed up a line so badly that Morgan quit singing and burst into laughter. Soon they were both laughing so hard they had tears running down their cheeks. Emily couldn't even remember the last time she'd laughed like that.

"You know what?" gasped Morgan.

"No, what?" Emily wiped the tears from her face and tried to catch her breath.

"You sing just like a white girl!"

And they both exploded into fits of laughter all over again.

chapter three

"You live in America now," Amy yelled. "Just speak English!" She slammed the front door behind her, but not quickly enough to avoid hearing her mother say, "Don't speak ill of your elders," only she said it in Vietnamese — *not* English, naturally! Amy couldn't understand her parents at all. Sure, they wanted *her* to act and talk and look just like an American girl, but it seemed *they* hardly tried to fit into this country at all. And they'd been here for years and years. Sometimes Amy wondered why they even bothered moving here in the first place. Oh, she wasn't stupid. She knew it had to do with "hard times after the war," but that meant little to her since she'd spent her whole life as an American.

Sometimes her family was so humiliating. Okay, not her older brother and sisters so much. At least they spoke English — even if it wasn't perfect. And for the most part they tried to fit in. But sometimes her parents were so old-fashioned and just plain weird that she actually pretended she didn't even know them. She knew that was a horrible way for a daughter to act, but sometimes they just made her crazy!

She checked her watch. It was already 7:48, and she did not like going to school even three minutes later than usual. She liked to be early and prepared and ready. Miss Thurman liked it too. She always smiled and treated Amy special when she was the first one to arrive. Sometimes she even gave her small jobs to do. Otherwise, Amy would carefully sort through her desk, sharpen her pencils, and then read until school finally began at eight thirty. Leaving even five minutes later than usual might really mess up her day. As she walked toward the entrance, she peered over at the street outside the trailer park, looking over to where the gang of mean boys liked to hang out, but no one was there. For a split second she considered heading off to school without the other three girls.

"Hey, Amy," yelled Carlie from her front porch just a few feet away. Carlie had a toddler balanced on one hip. "This is my little brother, Pedro." The small boy smiled and waved at her, then Carlie set him back inside the house. "*Adios, mijo,*" she called as she closed the door. Then she grabbed up her backpack and ran over to where Amy was waiting for her.

"Do you have any brothers or sisters?" asked Carlie as she slipped her backpack over her shoulder.

"Yes, I have two sisters and a brother, but they're a *lot* older than me." She pointed to a mobile home across the street. "They live in their own house right there. They're

all still single and in their twenties. They work at our restaurant part-time and go to college part-time."

"Wow, they have their own house to live in. That must
be so neat."

"Yeah, but believe me, it can be a real pigpen too. Still,
I guess they have fun together." Of course, Amy wished
they would include her in their fun, but sometimes the gulf
between her and her siblings seemed wider than the whole
Pacific Harbor. She glanced at her watch again as they
waited by the entrance to the trailer park, tapping her foot
with impatience. Where were the other two girls?

Amy watched as Carlie tried several times to put a barrette in her hair, but it kept popping back open. "Amy," she
finally said, "can you snap this stupid thing shut for me?"

Amy set down her book bag to help. "The barrette's
too small, I think. Or maybe your hair's too big." She
struggled to push the mane of black curls into the barrette,
then finally she pushed so hard that it broke into three
pieces. "I'm so sorry, Carlie." She handed over the broken
pieces and looked down at her feet. She felt foolish for
not being able to do such a simple task. Carlie probably
thought she was really dumb.

"Oh, it's okay, Amy. It was just a crummy old barrette
anyway. I only wanted to get my hair back away from my
face. I wish I could cut this mop-top off. I'd love to have
hair like yours, Amy."

"Really?" Amy patted her bobbed hair as she studied Carlie's long curls. "I think your hair is pretty, Carlie. I don't know why you'd want to cut it."

"Because it would feel so good not to have it hanging all over the place. And it makes me too hot. Plus it takes forever to dry it after I wash it. But my parents think girls should have long hair. Period. No argument."

Amy nodded. "My parents have some strange ideas too," she admitted. "I sort of know what you mean."

"Hey there!" called Morgan as she and Emily jogged over to meet them. "Sorry we're late. It was my fault. My mom wanted to meet Emily, and I made Emily come in for a minute ... well ... it was supposed to be just a minute. But then you don't know my mom."

"She's really nice," chimed in Emily. Amy looked at Emily. She seemed happier today. Her blue eyes seemed brighter. Amy looked at Emily's pants and was surprised to see that they were the same jeans from yesterday, only with some weird kind of patch on the knee.

"So, you fixed that hole in your jeans," said Amy in what she knew was her snippy tone of voice. The words were barely out before she regretted saying them. Still, that's just how it was with her: sometimes things popped out of her mouth that sounded all wrong. It was like she couldn't stop it even if she tried. And then sometimes she just didn't bother to try.

"Morgan fixed them for me," said Emily. "Didn't she do a good job?"

Amy nodded slightly then started walking. "Come on, you slowpokes, we need to get going. I've never been this late for school. Not ever!" She wondered if Miss Thurman missed her.

Carlie quickly caught up with her. "Boy, Amy, sometimes you act like such a snob." Amy looked at her from the corner of her eye. Fortunately, Carlie was smiling, and so Amy decided not to get mad.

"I know," she admitted. "It's like I can't help it. Sometimes the words just come out wrong. And then it's too late."

"Well, you can always apologize."

"I suppose. But that's kind of like saying that I'm wrong."

"Well, aren't you?"

"Maybe, but I don't *like* being wrong."

Carlie shook her head and muttered something in Spanish.

"Hey, this is America. *Speak English!*" demanded Amy. Carlie just laughed.

"Don't look now," said Morgan from behind. "But I think our friend Derrick's up ahead."

Amy peered up the street to see the edge of a bike tire and a flash of red hair protruding from the corner of a fence. "Do you think he's alone?" whispered Amy, wishing she and Carlie weren't the ones walking in front just now.

"Hey, I thought I told you trailer trash to stay off our turf!" he yelled as he popped out from behind the fence just a few feet in front of them.

Amy froze in her tracks. She wanted to move, but her feet felt superglued to the sidewalk. Carlie tugged on her sleeve to continue.

"Come on, Amy," encouraged Morgan as she and Emily kept walking, moving right past Amy. "We need to get to school. We're late, remember?"

Amy took one step and then another. Carlie was still holding on to her sleeve, actually pulling her along. Amy knew she shouldn't let Derrick see that he was getting to her, but she couldn't help it. She looked down, deciding to distract herself by counting the cracks in the sidewalk as she put one foot in front of the other. Maybe after a few hundred cracks they'd all be safely at school. Then a tire screech in front of her made her look up — right into the sneering face of Derrick Smith. He was so close she could almost count the freckles on his pudgy face.

"I *said*, I don't want no dumb trailer-park kids walking on my turf. Are you deaf or something, girlie? What's wrong? Are you like your parents — can't speak English?"

Amy really wanted to say something hurtful and mean, but it felt like someone had locked her lips shut. She looked into his mean face again. How dare he say that about her family? She actually wanted to hit him. Instead, she began to cry.

All three girls gathered around Amy now. They stood in a half circle as if to hold the bully off. But at this point, Amy no longer cared. She was too humiliated to care.

"Derrick Smith, you are such a complete idiot!" yelled Morgan. "You don't own this street, and if you don't get out of our way, you're going to be sorry."

"Whatcha gonna do? Beat me up?"

"You'd be the laughingstock of town if you got beat up by a bunch of sixth-grade girls, now, wouldn't you?" said Carlie as she took a step closer. Emily followed on the left, and Morgan closed in from the right. They had nearly surrounded him now. Then Carlie started swinging her backpack slowly back and forth, almost as if it were a weapon. And then Emily did the same. All Amy could do was stand there and stare like a total coward. She wished that the sidewalk would open up and swallow her whole. And then an amazing thing happened — Derrick Smith backed off.

"Just you watch out, you trailer-park hicks. I'm not finished with you yet."

They all cheered as he rode off. Everyone except for Amy. She still had tears streaming down her cheeks and was searching her book bag for her little plastic package of Kleenex that didn't seem to be there.

"Here, Amy." Emily quietly handed her a slightly rumpled tissue from her own pocket.

Amy wiped her eyes and blew her nose. Emily placed a gentle hand on her shoulder without saying anything. Amy was glad Emily didn't speak. The whole incident was so embarrassing. How ridiculous she must look, crying over some creepy boy's stupid comments. Just because he made fun of her or her family or where she lived. How totally ignorant she must seem!

And yet, how words could hurt. Words could really hurt.

The foursome walked home together after school. No one needed to be reminded of their pact, and no one complained about waiting for Morgan while she ran back inside to pick up her gym clothes. None of them wanted to meet up with the gang alone. Especially not after Derrick's threat this morning.

"Don't you just hate it when they call us the 'trailer-park kids' as if that makes us second-class citizens?" said Carlie. "I'd just like to smack that Derrick Smith right in his big red nose!" She swung her backpack for emphasis.

"I know what you mean," agreed Morgan. "As if living in that crummy apartment complex on Oak Street makes him better than us. I'd just like to know what makes him so mean and stupid."

"Maybe his dog got rabies and died," offered Carlie.

"Or maybe his mom is a really bad cook," suggested Emily with a half smile.

Morgan laughed. "Or maybe his father hangs him by his toenails in the cellar every night."

"Maybe he *should*," said Amy. Then they all laughed.

Carlie was glad to see that Amy had recovered from this morning. She could tell that she'd been embarrassed, and Carlie had felt really sorry for her, but she hadn't known what to do or say. She'd been so relieved when Emily stepped in.

"You know," began Carlie in a serious voice, "sometimes my friends and I would get teased back where I used to live. But that was because there were only a few Latino families in our town, you know, and we were the only minority. Do you think that's why the gang is picking on us now?"

"I thought so at first," admitted Morgan. "But then I noticed the gang has a Hispanic guy, Enrico Valdez, who hangs out with them sometimes. Plus, yesterday they attacked Emily, and she's not exactly a minority."

"Not unless you count poor white trash," Emily spoke quietly.

"Emily, that's not true," Carlie declared. "None of us are trash. Like my parents say, we're all just passing through. Sometimes we come upon hard times, but that doesn't mean things won't change someday. *Right?*"

"Right," agreed Morgan.

"Besides," stated Amy, "just because you live in Harbor View Mobile-Home Court doesn't mean you're poor. For instance, my parents could afford a better place, but they don't want to move. They like where we live."

"Really?" asked Carlie in disbelief. She knew her mother wanted to move to a bigger house. They'd left a really pretty home back in Coswell, one that was twice as big as where they lived now.

"Yes." Amy seemed to hold her head a little higher as she continued. "Our house is actually quite nice. It looks much better on the inside. In fact, why don't you all come over to see it? How does Saturday sound?"

So they all agreed to go to Amy's at two on the following day. Carlie was curious about what they would do there, but she was glad for the invitation. And, as strange as it seemed, the four of them had suddenly become sort of a team or something. After several weeks of not having one single friend, she now felt like she had three. And each one seemed pretty nice and interesting too. She looked down the street again, in search of the gang of bullies that had driven them together, but nothing unusual caught her eye.

"You know, this hanging together works pretty good for going to school," she admitted to the girls. "But what'll we do when we have to do something alone? I sure don't want to face Derrick by myself." Just the thought made Carlie's stomach twist.

"Good question, Carlie," Morgan frowned and pushed her glasses up on her nose. "I wouldn't like to run into them on my own either. It's almost like this whole thing is getting way out of hand. I sort of wonder if we should tell someone —" But her words were cut short as two guys on bikes zipped up. Fortunately, Derrick was not one of them. This time it was Jeff and Enrico.

"Derrick told us to tell you to stay off our turf," said Jeff without much enthusiasm, almost as if he were delivering a message from a teacher.

"Oh, we're so surprised," said Carlie sarcastically. "We just never would've guessed it."

"Look, we're not trying to start anything," said Jeff. "We just wanted to warn you."

"Warn us about what?" demanded Morgan. "That you big, tough seventh graders are going to beat up a bunch of girls who are younger than you? Now, that's really tough. I'm, like, so impressed!"

Jeff looked over his shoulder. Enrico said nothing. His eyes met Carlie's, then quickly looked away.

Carlie felt a miniature volcano bubbling up inside her, and finally it exploded. "I just do not understand you, Enrico. Where I came from we stuck together when the gringos picked on us. You are a traitor, Enrico! My father would spit on you." She felt her cheeks grow hot. She halfway wished she could take back her fiery words.

"Come on, Jeff. Let's get outta here," said Enrico as he turned his bike around. "This is stupid." Jeff just shook his head and followed.

"Wow," said Carlie, hardly daring to believe her eyes. The bullies were actually leaving. The other girls slapped her on the back.

"Way to go, Carlie!" Morgan gave her a high five. "You really told those two off. Maybe they'll come to their senses now, and maybe they'll lose dumb old Derrick completely."

They celebrated all the way home. And while Carlie was really relieved that their persecution was over — at least for the moment — she hoped this wouldn't be the end of these new friendships. She liked hanging with her new friends and hoped they'd find other reasons to stick together.

"You know, this place really is pretty ugly," noticed Morgan as she stopped to look at the entrance of the mobile-home park.

"What do you mean?" asked Amy.

"Harbor View Mobile-Home Court. I mean, just look at it. It really does seem kinda slummy. See that broken-down fence over there … and there are weeds and black-berry vines all over the place. And look at all the litter everywhere." She pointed to the sign at the entrance. It was missing the letter $\mathcal{V}$. "It says Harbor *iew*," she said, making a face. "Pretty pathetic." All the girls stopped and stared. And for a long moment, no one said anything.

Carlie had noticed all these same things the very first day they'd moved in here, but slowly she'd sort of gotten used to them. And recently, with the help of her dad, she'd started to create her own special place—a little getaway that helped her to forget about some of the ugliness. "Hey," she said suddenly. "I want to show you guys something." She started jogging toward her house. "Come with me."

And without even asking her why, the girls came, following her right up to her house. But instead of going in through her front door, she led them around the outside of the house. For one thing, she knew that Pedro and Miguel might still be napping, but besides that, she knew this would make for a better entrance. Then she pushed back the little metal gate that her father had put up and took them into her backyard.

There in the center was the little patch of patio that she and her dad had made themselves with cement paving blocks that he'd managed to scrounge from a demolition site. Surrounding the patio were colorful clay pots of different sizes and shapes, ones that her grandmother had given her. And each one was filled with an assortment of pretty spring flowers and small shrubs. A wooden bench that they'd brought from their old yard was set off to the side. Nearby was a picnic table and chairs. But to the right stood her pride and joy—a fountain that she and Dad had put together themselves. And, as usual, it was bubbling and gurgling with water tumbling down the sides.

"This is so beautiful," said Amy, dipping her fingertips into the water that flowed from the fountain.

"It's like a secret paradise," said Morgan, sitting down on the bench. Emily nodded with wide eyes, drinking it all in. Suddenly Carlie felt so pleased and proud. Papa had helped, but this whole thing had truly been her idea.

She'd hated leaving their lovely home in Coswell, but the hardest part of all was losing their beautiful backyard and garden. Papa had promised she could make another special place, but at first she thought it was hopeless. The yard was so small and overgrown with weeds. But then she'd rolled up her sleeves and started investing most of her free time out here working in the dirt. Tia Maria donated lots of flowers from her own garden, and Carlie had used her babysitting money to purchase others. She loved being outside, and working in the garden was the one time when she was allowed to get dirty and didn't have to act like such a lady.

At first, Carlie had been worried that her new friends might think it was lame for her to enjoy working in a garden, but it truly was what she loved most of all. And someday she hoped to own her own landscaping business. But that was a secret she kept to herself, at least for now.

"I just got an idea," exclaimed Morgan, jumping up from the bench. "Why don't we do for the trailer park what Carlie has done for this yard?"

"Oh, that would be a lot of work," said Carlie.

"Well, it wouldn't have to be *this* nice," explained Morgan. "I just mean we could clean it up some. You know, make it look better. Improve it."

"Yeah," chimed in Emily. "If we all worked together, we might be able to make it look a lot nicer. Then maybe we wouldn't get teased so much for living here."

Amy nodded. "Maybe we could plant a couple of trees or something by the entrance. Paint that cruddy-looking fence."

Before long they were all full of ideas. Some sounded pretty good, and others pretty impossible. But Carlie was getting excited. Maybe this would give them a way to work together — to become real friends.

"When you come to my house tomorrow," said Amy importantly, "We can all sit down and have a real planning session about how to do these things."

"Great idea," said Morgan. "Maybe we should make Carlie here the leader, since she knows so much about gardens and stuff."

Carlie felt her face grow warm, partly with pride, partly with embarrassment. She'd never been a leader of anything. "Oh, I don't think we really need a leader. Why don't we all just help out."

So it was agreed. They would meet at Amy's at ten. And for now they wouldn't have an official leader. After the girls left, Carlie sat down on the bench. Maybe moving to this town wasn't so bad after all. Today had been one of the best days she could remember since coming here.

She picked a bright yellow pansy and looked into its sweet, dark face. It looked so hopeful and full of promise. It was sort of how she felt. She rubbed the velvety surface against her cheek and thought about how good it was to be in a garden, and how much the green growing things reminded her of God.

Maybe putting some of these growing things around the mobile-home park would remind some other people about God too. Carlie wondered what her friends would think of *that* idea.

chapter five

Morgan chattered away as she and Emily walked to Amy's house on Saturday. "… And then I thought we could earn money to buy flowers and stuff by collecting returnable pop cans. The store will give us five cents per can. I bet we could get fifty cans just from the residents here." She tossed her silent friend a quick sideways glance. Emily just nodded. It bugged Morgan that Emily was so quiet, but she figured that maybe she was just like that. Or maybe she was what Grandma called moody. But it didn't matter. Not really. She liked Emily, and they were friends. That was all that mattered.

"Hey there," called Carlie as she bounded down the steps of her porch toward them.

"What are you all dressed up for, Carlie?" asked Morgan, eyeing Carlie's outfit: a pink T-shirt and a matching ruffled skirt.

Carlie's face darkened. "My mother," she muttered.

"What do you mean?"

"My mother thought I should look nice to go to Amy's. She thinks we're having a party or something. I tried to explain, but I couldn't make her understand."

Carlie looked down at her clothes and frowned.

"Well, it's no big deal, Carlie. I mean, you do look pretty. I just ... " Morgan felt sorry that she'd made Carlie uncomfortable. "My grandma would think you look the way girls should look," she added. "She's always trying to get me to wear stuff like that."

"Well, you're lucky you get to dress the way you want to."

"Yeah, I'd probably go nuts if I couldn't wear what I like." She looked down at her tie-dyed T-shirt, faded jeans, and well-worn sandals: not exactly a style statement, but comfortable. She glanced at Emily. She had remained quiet throughout their little fashion discussion, and now Morgan noticed Emily had on the same patched jeans again. In fact, as Morgan thought about it, it seemed to her that Emily wore those pants every day.

"Come on in, you guys," called Amy, throwing open the door. The girls entered a spacious living room with dark blue carpet and some Asian-looking furniture, including low, dark coffee tables and large ceramic vases. Even the art on the wall looked Asian. Amy proudly gave them a quick tour of the whole house. As Amy had said, it was much better on the inside, very fancy. It was also very tidy — not a single thing looked out of place.

"Are you the only one home?" asked Carlie.

"No, my mother's here. She's fixing us something."

"Where is she?" asked Morgan. "I didn't see her."

"Well, she's probably trying to stay out of our way."

Morgan looked curiously at Amy. It was hard to imagine the kind of mother who would want to stay out of the way. Morgan's mother always wanted to be involved in everything.

"Why don't we go to my room," said Amy. "My desk is in there, and we can write down our plans for fixing up Harbor View."

Amy's room was lavender and white, and everything seemed to match perfectly. But Morgan didn't like it much. She thought it lacked creativity. Naturally, she kept this to herself as she looked at the row of porcelain dolls on top of Amy's long, white mirrored dresser. They all looked so straight and stiff, as if they belonged in some weird kind of doll army.

"Sit down," said Amy, pointing to her bed. The three girls sat stiffly on the lavender-and-white bedspread, as if they were afraid to wrinkle it. Amy sat at her neat white desk and pulled out a pad of paper and a pencil. Of course, these items were lavender too. And for some reason this made Morgan giggle.

"What's so funny?" asked Amy.

"Oh, nothing really." But Morgan couldn't stop. And soon Emily was smiling and she started to giggle too.

"*What is it?*" demanded Amy, slamming the little lavender notebook down on her desk.

"I'm sorry," said Morgan between giggles. "It's just that everything is so ... so ... lavender." She burst into full-blown laughter now, and Emily did the same, holding her hand over her mouth as if to stop herself. Carlie and Amy just stared at them like they thought the two girls were crazy.

"Is something wrong with lavender?" asked Amy. "Or are you two just losing it?"

"No, no, lavender's fine." Morgan took off her glasses and wiped her eyes, careful not to look at Emily lest she burst out laughing again.

"Well, I think your room is pretty, Amy," stated Carlie.

"Thanks." Amy frowned at Morgan. "Now let's start thinking about what we want to do to fix up the trailer park."

"We have to plant flowers in front by the sign...."

"Yeah, and the sign needs to be repainted."

"How about a couple of trees by the sign?"

"What about that old rickety fence?"

"Hold it!" yelled Amy. "I am not getting this all down. Slow down. One at a time, and wait until I call on you."

"Okay, teacher," joked Morgan.

Amy tossed her one of her snooty looks, but Morgan just laughed. The girls slowly told her their ideas, and before long they had a pretty good list. And when

Amy read the whole thing back to them, they were quite impressed with themselves.

"But that was the easy part," said Morgan. "Now we need to figure out how we can raise some money. I had a couple of ideas, like collecting pop cans to turn in for money and old newspapers to sell to the recycling center."

"We could have a huge garage sale," offered Carlie. "My mother loves garage sales."

"How about a lemonade stand?" suggested Amy. "We could sell cookies too. Hey, speaking of food, I bet it's ready."

"What's that?" asked Carlie.

"Come on and see." Amy led them to the dining room where a small feast was laid on the big dark table. Everything was neatly arranged with pretty plates and napkins. There were almond cookies and sesame cakes, and fresh fruit arranged prettily on a plate. There was also a pot of tea and four tiny cups.

"This looks like a tea party," exclaimed Carlie.

"That was really nice of your mother." Morgan looked around, but still didn't see anyone in the kitchen.

They ate and visited and continued to plan the steps it would take to transform Harbor View Mobile-Home Court into a place where anyone would be proud to live.

"But there's one important thing we need to do first," said Morgan between bites. "It won't be easy, but we need to talk to Mr. Greeley."

"Who's that?" asked Emily.

"Didn't you meet him when you moved in? He's the manager of Harbor View. Or maybe he's the owner. I'm not sure. Anyway, he runs this place."

"Not very well," added Amy as she refilled her cup with tea.

"Obviously," agreed Morgan. "But the problem is, he's sort of grumpy—"

"Not *sort of*," interrupted Carlie. "He can be downright mean and nasty. When my dad wanted to put a little fence around our yard just to keep Pedro and Miguel off the street, Mr. Greeley acted like we were going to destroy the place. All we wanted to do was make it nicer."

"And then whenever you need Mr. Greeley," continued Amy, "he's never around. If something's broken or needs attention, the old geezer just totally disappears. It drives my parents crazy!"

"My grandma thinks it's because he's sad," said Morgan.

"Or crazy," said Amy. "My parents think he has mental problems."

"Anyway, we need to figure out a way to get Mr. Greeley to listen to us," said Morgan. "And to agree to our plan." She thought for a moment. "My grandma always says you can get more flies with honey than with vinegar."

"What does *that* mean?" asked Amy.

"Well, it means we should be sweet to Mr. Greeley, like honey, in order to get him to agree to our ideas. I don't know … it's just a silly old saying. My grandma has lots of them."

Carlie nodded. "I get you. My parents have some sayings like that too, and they don't make any sense, but they still say them — usually in Spanish."

Morgan held up an almond cookie. "How about if we take Mr. Greeley some of these cookies, Amy? That's sort of like honey."

So it was agreed, and they all marched over to Mr. Greeley's with a bag full of the delicious almond cookies. Morgan was nominated to speak. She didn't mind since she'd known Mr. Greeley the longest, and she wasn't too afraid of him. Well, at least not when she had backups like today. His double-wide house was part office. It could've been nice looking, but it was dirty and dingy and had boxes of all kinds of stuff stacked around on the front porch. A scrawny-looking tiger cat rubbed against Morgan's legs, and she reached over to stroke its back. The cat purred loudly and rubbed again. She doubted that Mr. Greeley ever petted the poor animal. It looked as if he hardly ever fed it.

"Wha'd'ya kids think you're doing on my porch?" called a gruff voice from around the corner. Mr. Greeley walked up with a sour-looking expression and a broken piece of glass in his hand. He did look pretty scary with wild wisps of uneven gray hair poking out from under a dusty old ball cap.

"We … uh … we just wanted to talk with you," began Morgan.

"'Bout what?" He scowled up at her.

"Well, first of all, we wanted to share some cookies with you." She reached over the porch railing and handed him the small bag of cookies. Her smile was met with a suspicious frown.

"What for?" He set down the piece of glass and looked into the bag.

"We just want to be neighborly. And we want to talk to you about an idea we have — an idea about fixing up Harbor View."

He scowled at her. "What are you talking about? Wha'd'ya mean by fixing it up?"

"We mean we'd just like to beautify the trailer court so that—"

"Just how d'ya kids think you're gonna *beautify* the court?" He pulled out a cookie, sniffed it, then took a cautious bite.

"We've made a list of ideas … "

Amy held out their list, keeping her distance like she thought the old man might have cooties or something.

He snatched the paper from her and quickly glanced down at it. "Yeah, well, that might sound fine and good to you little girls. But who's gonna foot the bill? I got no money for silly frills like that."

"We thought we could raise some money," said Carlie in a meek voice.

He rubbed his grizzly whiskered chin and grunted. "Hmm. Well, I don't want you making no messes. You mess anything up, you break anything, and I'll have your parents pay. And don't think I won't."

Morgan wondered how they could possibly make things look any worse than they already were, but she just nodded solemnly. "No, sir, we won't mess anything up. We only want to make it nicer."

"What for?" He peered straight into her eyes as if he suspected they might be up to some kind of mischief.

"We just want to live in a place that looks pretty. That's all."

"Humph," he grunted. *"Pretty!"* He shook his head and walked away. "Just don't you mess nothing up, ya hear?" he called over his shoulder.

"Sure thing, Mr. Greeley." Morgan gave the other girls a thumbs-up sign.

"You did it, Morgan!" Carlie gave her a high five.

Morgan smiled. "Yep, now we just better make sure we 'don't mess nothing up,'" she said in a deep Mr.

Greeley-type voice. The girls laughed.

"Should we start today?" asked Emily. "I mean, we could probably begin by pulling some weeds and picking up trash and stuff."

"Great idea, Em," agreed Morgan. "I'll go get some trash bags, and we can start out front by the entrance. Maybe if some of the folks around here see what we're up to, they'll want to help out too."

chapter six

It was hard work, but working together made it seem almost like fun. Morgan turned it into a game, seeing who could fill up their bags the fastest. And before long the whole entrance was free of weeds and trash. It looked a little bare and plain, but at least it was neater and cleaner.

"Not bad for a couple hours of work," announced Carlie as she stood up and leaned on her rake. Her dad had provided the group with tools and encouragement, and they had managed to fill four huge garbage bags. "Hey, here comes Mr. Greeley." The girls waved at him as he strolled toward them.

He surveyed their work with a creased forehead then grumbled, "You just make sure you get those garbage bags into the trash. There's supposed to be high winds off the Harbor tonight. Don't want that stuff blowing all over the place." He turned out of the entrance and continued walking toward town.

"Man, he didn't even say thanks," exclaimed Morgan, removing her glasses to wipe the gritty sweat from her forehead.

"And he didn't even say it looked better. Is he blind or something?" Carlie tied off the top of her bag and brushed the dirt off her hands. She no longer wore the pretty pink outfit, but instead had on shorts and a T-shirt, and her hair was pulled back in a ponytail.

"You girls need some refreshments?" called a woman's voice. They looked up to see Morgan's mom walking their way with some bottles of juice. "I've got ice-cold 'passion fruit – strawberry' or 'melon madness' to choose from."

"Thanks, Mom." Morgan took the drinks and handed them to her friends, introducing Carlie and Amy. Her mom had met Emily already.

"Thanks for the drink, Mrs. Evans," said Amy politely.

"You're sure welcome. You can call me Cleo. It makes me feel like an old woman to be called Mrs. Evans. And I'd like to still think I'm young. Say, it looks like you girls are doing a fantastic job here. I'm impressed."

Carlie sniffed. "Well, Mr. Greeley didn't seem very impressed. He just came by to make sure we threw the bags in the trash bin so the stuff doesn't get blown all over the place again."

Cleo laughed. "That's just his way, Carlie. He's not what you'd call a happy camper. But I'm sure, deep down he appreciates what you're doing."

"Maybe really deep, deep down. So deep that even he doesn't know it," suggested Morgan.

"So, what are you girls going to do next?"

"Flowers!" exclaimed Carlie, throwing her arms into the air. "We need to plant lots and lots of flowers. But first we've got to earn some money to buy them." She kicked the toe of her tennis show in the dry dirt. "And we can't wait too long. Because it'll start getting warmer soon, and we'll miss the best part of the growing season."

"Next week should be our money-drive week," said Morgan.

"Yeah," chimed in Amy, turning to Morgan's mom with a big smile. "We made a list of ways to make money. Maybe we should get started right away."

"We could start collecting pop cans tomorrow." Morgan glanced at her mom. "After church, that is."

Cleo smiled. "I wonder if any of your friends would be interested in visiting our church, Morgan. Remember, we have that special music group coming tomorrow."

Morgan's eyes lit up and she turned to her friends. "Oh, yeah. It's this really cool group of college kids from Canada, and they sing and do skits and stuff. You'd probably like it — if you want to come."

"It sounds like fun, but we usually go to Mass on Sunday," said Carlie. "Mass is sort of boring, but we always go out for pizza afterward."

Amy scratched her head. "You know, I don't think I've ever been to church before. Not that I can remember anyway. It sounds sort of interesting. And I do like music."

"Great, you want to come then? How about you, Emily?"

Emily's cheeks grew red. "Well, it sounds nice —"

"Great then," interrupted Morgan. "It's settled. Be ready by nine thirty tomorrow morning, and we'll pick you up. Now let's go dump these bags before Mr. Greeley has a cow."

After they threw the bags into the trash bin, Emily and Morgan walked back to their end of the park together. Emily was quiet again, and Morgan wanted to ask her what was wrong. Instead, she invited her to come home with her.

"I want you to see how that dress turned out," she told Emily. "You remember the batik material? I just finished it last night, and it's so cool, you've just got to see it."

"I'll bet it looks great," said Emily as she followed Morgan into the house.

Morgan pulled the dress out of the closet. "The hemline looks uneven," she explained, just as she'd done with Grandma. "But it's supposed to be like that."

"It looks really good, Morgan. I bet it'll be even cuter on." Emily collapsed into Morgan's beanbag chair and sighed. She looked tired. Morgan suspected it wasn't from working so hard today.

"What's wrong, Em?" Morgan sat on the futon across from her. "I can tell that something's bugging you. Did I do anything to make you mad? I mean, I know how I sometimes say things too quickly. I hope I didn't hurt your feelings. Mom is always telling me to think before I speak—"

"No, Morgan. Nothing like that." Emily sighed again.

"Well, what then? You can tell me, Emily. I'm your friend. Maybe I can do something to help."

Emily shook her head. "I don't see how."

"Well, you'll never know if you don't talk to me. You know this is exactly what friends are for." Morgan fingered the braids in her hair. "I haven't had a really good friend since Mom and I moved here to live with Grandma. I was sort of hoping that you and I could become good friends, ya know?"

Emily leaned her head back and closed her eyes, but Morgan could tell by the way her eyebrows were pulled together that something was upsetting her.

"Come on," urged Morgan. "You can trust me. Tell me what's wrong."

"Maybe that's it." She opened her eyes and sat up straight again, looking as if she were studying Morgan, trying to figure out whether she could really trust her. Morgan smiled hopefully. "I guess I'm getting tired of pretending like nothing's wrong," said Emily. "Maybe I should just tell you."

"Yes," agreed Morgan. "My grandma says you always feel better after you get things out into the open."

"But you have to promise not to tell anyone," said Emily. "Can I trust you?"

"Of course!"

"Okay ..." Emily took in a deep breath. "And the truth is I think I might actually explode or something if I don't talk to someone. I write lots of stuff in my diary, but it's not the same as talking to someone real." She tugged a loose piece of rubber on the edge of her tennis shoes, snapping it again and again.

"Well, I'm real, and I'm listening."

"Yeah." Emily leaned back into the beanbag again, sinking in almost as if she wanted it to swallow her. "Where to begin?" she muttered. "Well, first of all, I was going to make up some lame excuse about not being able to go to church with you tomorrow."

"Why?" asked Morgan. "Are you an atheist? Or some other kind of religion? Our church is actually what you call nondenominational, so it doesn't really matter if you're a Baptist or Methodist or whatever-ist, Em. It's pretty small, but it's full of cool people who —"

"No, that's not it. I was just thinking of an excuse, because ... well, I don't even have a dress to wear."

"Oh, that's okay. People wear anything they want. Even jeans."

"Really?" Emily sat up and looked slightly hopeful now.

"Of course. It doesn't matter what you wear. It only matters that you go. But is that really what was bugging you? Wow! I thought, like, maybe you had some really awful horrible problem or something. Like your mom's an ax-murderer, or you're hiding a wanted felon in your basement." Morgan laughed. "Guess you don't have a basement, huh?"

Emily bit her lip. And suddenly Morgan realized that maybe Emily did have some horrible kind of problem. Morgan didn't want to be too pushy. In some ways, Emily seemed kind of fragile, like a girl who had been through a lot. Morgan had been through some hard things herself. And she knew that talking about it was hard. Maybe Emily didn't completely trust Morgan yet. So they just talked about silly things and listened to music, and after a while Emily went home.

Morgan stood by the window and watched as Emily walked away from her house. She could tell by the slump of her shoulders that Emily was carrying a heavy load. Still, Morgan wasn't sure how she could help. And so she prayed. She asked God to help her be sensitive to Emily's feelings. And if there was anything she could do to help, she prayed that God would help her to do it.

"Why didn't you invite Emily to stay for dinner?" asked Grandma from behind her.

"Huh?" Morgan turned around and stared at Grandma. "Why?"

"Why?" Grandma laughed. "Why not?" Then she put her hand on Morgan's shoulder. "I was talking to Emily's mother just a few days ago. I introduced myself to her out by the trash bin. Mrs. Adams told me that she works a lot of hours at the new resort. She and her eighteen-year-old son are both employed there. And she mentioned how Emily is on her own quite a bit. She seemed concerned about Emily being alone in the evening."

"Well, why didn't you say so?" said Morgan.

"So give her a call," suggested Grandma. "See if she likes ribs."

"Who doesn't like ribs?" said Morgan as she reached for the phone. Then she stopped. "Hey, I don't even know Emily's phone number."

Grandma laughed. "That's why the good Lord gave you legs, honey. Now just run over there and fetch that sweet little girl back here."

Morgan dashed down the street and up the steps to Emily's house, knocking loudly on the door. All the shades were drawn, but she knew that Emily was home. Still, no one answered. "Emily!" she called loudly. "It's just me, Morgan. Open the door, will ya?" She knocked again, even louder this time. Surely, Emily could hear her now. Then finally she heard the deadbolt lock click, and the door opened just wide enough for Emily to stick her nose out.

"Say, girl, I was starting to get seriously worried. Why didn't you answer the door?" Morgan scolded her.

"Oh," said Emily, opening the door just a little wider. "Sorry." She frowned, but didn't ask Morgan to come in.

"What's wrong?" Morgan asked, noticing that Emily's eyes looked red and her cheeks were wet. Morgan looked over Emily's shoulder, noticing that the living room behind her was completely empty of any furnishings. "Are you okay, Emily? Can I come in?"

Emily opened the door and stepped back, allowing Morgan to come inside. But still, she didn't say anything. Something really did seem to be wrong. Maybe Emily wasn't supposed to let anyone in the house when her mom was gone.

"I was going to call you, Emily, but I don't have your number."

"We don't have a phone."

Morgan nodded. "Yeah, well, you guys haven't been here very long." She nodded toward the living room. "Looks like your furniture hasn't even arrived yet."

Emily didn't say anything.

Morgan glanced into the kitchen, noticing a box of cornflakes, a carton of milk, and a bowl on the counter. "That your dinner?"

"Yeah." Emily looked embarrassed.

Morgan nodded as she strolled into the kitchen and looked around. "Hey, I have cereal for dinner sometimes. Like when Grandma has bunco night."

Emily still didn't say anything.

Morgan peered at the bowl of cereal, noticing that there were white chunks of something on top.

"The milk was sour," said Emily, picking up the bowl and dumping the contents into the garbage disposal and turning it on.

"Well, that's good," said Morgan.

"Good?" Emily turned off the noisy appliance and just stared at Morgan.

"Yeah, Grandma's cooking ribs tonight, and you're joining us for dinner." She took Emily by the arm and began escorting her out. "You need to leave a note or anything?" Emily found a pencil and scratched a quick note on the back of an envelope, then silently followed Morgan out of the empty house.

"Grandma talked to your mom the other day," Morgan said as they walked toward her house. "So they've met and stuff. And your mom even told Grandma that she's been worried about you being home alone and stuff. So I'm sure she won't mind."

"She won't be home until after nine anyway," said Emily as they went inside.

After a great meal of ribs, corn, and buttermilk biscuits, with lemon meringue pie for dessert, they went to Morgan's room and sat down. Emily had been very quiet, but polite, during dinner. And although Morgan knew that it might just be because she was feeling shy, Morgan suspected it was something more. Something seemed to be troubling Emily, and Morgan wanted to find out what it was. They just sat there for a few minutes, Emily on the beanbag chair and Morgan on the futon. But neither girl spoke.

"That was a good dinner," Emily finally said in a sad little voice. "Thanks for asking me over."

"Better than cornflakes and sour milk?" teased Morgan. Then Emily started to cry.

"I'm sorry," Morgan said quickly. "I didn't mean to make you feel bad. I mean, I realize that something's wrong. And I really wish you'd talk to me about it, Emily. I think it would help to talk."

Emily nodded, wiping her tears away with the sleeve of her sweatshirt. "Yeah, I know..."

"I mean, it must be hard being new in town," said Morgan quickly. "And not having your stuff at your house yet. And—"

"My mom and dad never got along very good...," began Emily in a quiet voice. Morgan leaned closer to listen. "The truth is my dad was pretty mean." She looked at Morgan now, almost as if she expected her to be shocked or something.

"Yeah, that happens a lot, Emily."

"Mostly he was mean to my mom." She looked down at her lap. "Sometimes he would hit her. A lot."

Morgan nodded. "I'm sorry, Emily. That must've been really hard on you."

"Yeah … it was. And Mom tried to leave him a couple of times before, but we never got very far. He always came around and found us. And then he'd say he was really sorry. Then he'd give us stuff, and he would promise her that things were gonna be different." She sighed. "Then we'd go back home with him, and for a while it would be okay. But then something would happen, and Dad would get mad, and it would be bad again." She paused, closing her eyes as if she wanted to block it out. And suddenly Morgan wondered if she was making Emily remember things that were better off left behind.

"It's okay if you don't want to tell me everything, Emily. I mean, I don't want you to feel worse. Just tell me if it makes you feel better."

Emily took a breath. "Well, it got pretty bad this last time, Morgan. You see, my dad's an alcoholic, and he was on a really bad binge — you know when they just drink and drink. And he lost his job and just got meaner and meaner, acting like it was all my mom's fault for everything." She shook her head with an angry expression.

"That must've been horrible."

"Yeah. I don't know how my mom could stand it. Anyway, Kyle, my big brother, just got really mad at my dad one night — right after my dad had hit my mom — and he stood up to my dad. It was so scary, Morgan." She looked up with frightened eyes, almost as if she were reliving the whole thing. "I thought my dad might kill him or something. He was really drunk and acting crazy. Finally Dad went into the bathroom, and my mom grabbed her purse and told me and Kyle to sneak out the back and get into the car. She met us there, and we drove away. We drove out of the state and just kept driving until we got here, to Boscoe Bay, and then we stopped."

"Wow, that's amazing. Your mom must be really brave. So that's why you don't have any furniture or clothes or anything?"

Emily nodded. And she looked almost relieved, like maybe this was a story she needed to tell. But then she got a worried expression. "But, Morgan," she said suddenly. "You can't tell anyone about this. Okay? Our name isn't really Adams. Mom just decided we'd call ourselves that as we were driving here. I think it was because Kyle and I always used to watch the *Addams Family* on TV, and we'd been singing the song. I thought it made sense that we'd become the Adams family, since we're pretty weird too."

"I don't think you're weird."

"Thanks. But everything still seems pretty weird to me. I mean, one day, we were sort of like a normal family … well, at least we looked like a normal family. We had a nice house full of furniture and clothes and stuff. Then the next day, we had nothing and we were on the run. Not that I'd want to go back. I wouldn't. But it's just pretty weird, you know. Still, even though we're poor right now, at least we're not afraid all the time. I just hope my dad doesn't find us."

"Well, Boscoe Bay is about the most remote town on the planet; I don't think you have to worry too much about that."

"I hope not. I just wish things would start feeling more normal. I mean, it was great that my mom found a pretty good job at the resort, but she works all the time. My brother works there too. And as soon as they get paid, we'll start getting things. Still, it's hard right now."

"Yeah, but it's going to get better, Emily. I have a strong feeling that God has great plans for you."

"You really think so? Sometimes I wonder about God. We never really went to church much. I hope you're right though."

"I think I am," Morgan assured her. "Grandma says I have a pretty strong spiritual connection to God." She smiled sheepishly. "Not that I want to brag or anything."

"Well, I probably better go. My mom will be getting home soon."

"Be ready for church at nine thirty," called Morgan as she waved at Emily from her porch, watching until Emily made it safely back to her house.

chapter eight

The next morning, Emily seemed to be a little more cheerful as she rode to church with Morgan and her mom and grandma. Amy wasn't able to join them today. She had to help out in her family's restaurant since her sister had come down with the flu, but she promised to come another time.

"You didn't wear the new dress you made," observed Emily as they sat together in the backseat.

Morgan shrugged and rubbed her hands over her jeans. "I didn't feel like it today. It's so foggy and cool this morning, it seemed more like a blue-jeans day." She smiled.

Emily looked down at her own jeans, running her finger over the patch that Morgan had made.

"Besides, like I said, you can wear whatever you like at my church."

As usual, Morgan's mom parked the car behind the church, which was located at the end of a somewhat-run-down strip mall.

"It doesn't really look much like a church," Morgan explained as they got out. "But that's because it used to be a shoe store."

"But it's got a lot of soul," joked Grandma as they walked toward the back door.

Morgan normally sat in the front row. She grinned and greeted her church friends, pausing to introduce Emily to a few as they made their way down the center aisle. She hoped that Emily wouldn't feel too uncomfortable being here.

"I always sit up here," she whispered to her. "That's because when we first started going here, no one sat in the front row, and I always felt sorry for the pastor. It was like no one wanted to get very close to him — like they thought he had the chicken pox or something. So I decided to make it my special mission to sit right here." She nodded at some high school girls also sitting in the front row. "See, they always sit up here now too. And Pastor George likes it. He calls us the cheering section."

Morgan noticed that the college girls, as usual, were dressed pretty cool. She fingered one of her braids. She would've liked to have worn her new dress today. She knew that some of the girls might even have commented on it. They thought she had style. But knowing that Emily would be wearing blue jeans made her decide to dress down as well. Besides, as Grandma often reminded her, "church isn't a place for showing off."

"Good morning, everyone!" boomed a voice from up front, jarring Morgan back to the present. A young man with shaggy blond hair smiled at the congregation. "Isn't it great to be alive? And isn't it great to know the one who makes life worth living? My friends and I came all the way from Vancouver, British Columbia, to share about all the amazing things that God has done in our lives." Background music started up and the group began to sing. Morgan blinked her eyes in surprise. Boy, could they sing! This was like having a front-row seat at a first-rate concert.

"Aren't they great!" whispered Morgan after they finished their first song.

Emily nodded enthusiastically. "They're awesome, Morgan."

After a couple of songs, the group did a skit about a girl who decided to steal money from her parents and then run away from home. But the runaway, played by a pretty red-haired girl, only found hard times and bad luck. Finally she decided to return to her family. She thought her father might reject her and throw her back out. But instead he greeted her with open arms. Then the girl who played the role of the runaway explained how God was like that — always ready and waiting to invite his children back. She shared about how her own life had been a mess, but then God had straightened it out.

Morgan glanced at Emily, wondering if she was taking all this in. It seemed like, more than anything, Emily could use a heavenly Father right now. Would she be ready to invite him into her heart someday?

Finally the group sang their last song, and the blond guy began to speak into the microphone in a quiet voice. "Maybe you've known Jesus for your whole life, or maybe you're just meeting him for the first time today. It doesn't really matter. We're all his kids, and he's just waiting for each one of us to come to him and place our hearts in his hands."

Morgan glanced at Emily again, and she could tell that Emily was feeling nervous. Was it because God was knocking on the door of her heart? Or because she was in a strange church? Whatever it was, Morgan decided it was time to pray. She bowed her head and asked God to show Emily how much he loved her. God could do that. Morgan knew it.

"And it doesn't matter what condition our hearts are in," continued the man. "They can be heavy, or broken, or even full of all kinds of gunk. Jesus doesn't care. Because he can fix them. He can clean out the gunk, and he can make them better than new. And do you know why? Because he loves us. Because he wants to live in our hearts. All we need to do is just invite him in. If you want to invite him in again, or even for the first time, go ahead and stand up right where you are. Go ahead. He is waiting for you."

Without looking to the left or right, Morgan stood up. She knew she was doing it as much for Emily as for herself. But she meant it just the same. She had no problem inviting Jesus into her heart again and again and again. She knew that he was there all the time anyway. Nothing wrong with saying, "Make yourself comfortable, Jesus." Now, if only Emily would do the same.

Just then, Morgan felt a brush of movement next to her and from the corner of her eye, she could see that Emily had shifted in her seat. Morgan shut her eyes tight. She knew that this was Emily's decision. So she just stood there with her head bowed, praying for Emily and echoing the words to the prayer that the man in front was leading.

Then the prayer was done and Morgan could see that Emily was still seated. She sat down next to her and felt a wave of disappointment. It seemed that Emily, more than anyone Morgan knew, needed God in her life right now. Why hadn't she stood up?

After the service, without even waiting for Morgan, Emily stood up and left. Worried that something was wrong, Morgan followed and they ended up in the women's restroom.

"Are you okay?" Morgan asked Emily.

Emily nodded. But Morgan could see tears in Emily's eyes.

"What's wrong?" asked Morgan, seriously concerned for her new friend.

"I think I just invited Jesus into my heart," Emily whispered.

Morgan's eyes grew wide. "Really?"

Emily nodded again.

"But you didn't stand."

"I know." Emily frowned. "Does that mean it's not real?"

"No, of course it's real," said Morgan. "If you prayed, it's real."

"Oh, good." Then Emily really did begin to cry. But, unlike yesterday's tears, these looked like happy tears. Joyful tears! "It sure does feel like it's real," she said to Morgan.

"I'm so excited for you!" Morgan hugged her. "It'll be so great to have a best friend who's a Christian too! This is fantabulous!" She looked at Emily's tearstained face. Did Emily fully understand what she'd just done? Had she really meant it? "You're sure about this, aren't you? I mean, you really did *want* to invite Jesus into your heart, right?"

Emily sucked in her breath with a creased brow, as if she was really considering Morgan's question. Then finally she nodded. "Yeah, I really did. But it just seems so strange, you know. But like I said, I can feel that something is different inside me. It's kinda hard to explain."

"That's just how it is," said Morgan. "Having Jesus in your heart is kinda hard to explain. But you know it when it's real."

"Well, I *know* it." She smiled now. "And I actually feel pretty good, Morgan. In fact, I feel really great!"

"This is so fantastic, Em!" Morgan squeezed Emily's arm. "Let's go back to the sanctuary and talk to the band. I'll bet we can get their autographs. Maybe I can talk Mom into letting me get a CD for them to sign. Aren't they cool? I wish I could do something like this someday. Wouldn't it be fun?" Morgan tugged Emily toward the front where some other kids were already lining up to meet the band members.

"Thanks for bringing me here today, Morgan," said Emily with happy eyes. "This is so cool."

Morgan hugged her again. "Totally cool. Not only are we friends now, but we're sisters too. Sisters in the Lord, Emily!"

Emily grinned. "Awesome!"

As it turned out, Morgan's mom bought both girls a CD. "That way you can each have a different one," she said, handing the CDs to them while they were still standing in line. "Then you can trade off when you want to."

"And we can get them signed!" said Morgan. "Thanks, Mom!"

Emily thanked her too. Then she turned to Morgan. "Your mom is so cool."

Morgan nodded. "Yeah, I know."

The girls got their signatures and chatted happily as Morgan's mom drove them home. Then they were barely out of the car before they heard Carlie yelling.

"Morgan!" she called out, waving as she ran toward them. "Emily!"

"Hey, Carlie," said Morgan. "What's up? You look like you just won the lottery or something."

"Well, it's not quite that good," admitted Carlie. "But it is exciting. Tia Maria just told me some great news."

"What's that?" asked Emily.

"We can get plants for free!"

"Plants for free?" Morgan frowned. "What are you talking about?"

"To plant around the place," said Carlie. "My aunt said we just go to the forest-service station and ask for a permit. And then we can go into the woods and dig some things up that can be transplanted here."

"Really?"

"Yeah. And Dad said he'll even take us in his pickup to do it." She frowned. "But not until next weekend. We can't get the permit today anyway."

"Still, that's good news, Carlie," said Morgan. She looked over to where they'd cleared the garbage and weeds away. "It is looking pretty bare over there."

"So, let's all plan on going out in the woods with my dad next weekend," Carlie told them. "And prepare to get dirty!" She grinned, rubbing her hands together as if there was nothing better than getting dirty. "I'm going to call Amy and tell her the good news."

"Amy is working at the restaurant today," said Emily.

"Yeah, but did you hear that her dad got her a cell phone?"

"Her own cell phone?" Morgan tried not to feel jealous.

"Yeah." Carlie nodded. "She told him a little about the bullies, and he went out and got her a cell phone yesterday. He told her that she was to call the police if they ever bug us again."

"Really?" Morgan was surprised, not so much because Mr. Ngo had told Amy to call the police, but that Amy had told her parents. Morgan had hoped that this was something they could handle themselves.

"Maybe that's a good thing," said Emily. "Just in case that Derrick Smith tries to do something again."

"Yeah," agreed Morgan. "It wouldn't surprise me if he did."

"He's such a jerk," said Carlie. "I think we still need to be careful."

"So, do we all walk to school together again tomorrow?" asked Emily.

"Of course," said Morgan. "No use taking chances. Even if Amy does have a cell phone, we still need to stick together."

Carlie grinned. "Good."

"See you at 7:50," called Emily as she started walking toward her house.

Morgan smiled to herself as she went into her own house. As weird as it was, she almost hoped that the bullies weren't ready to give up yet. It seemed like it was their attacks that brought the girls together in the first place. Hopefully they could keep it up long enough that the girls would all be fast friends by the time summer vacation started.

chapter nine

"Are you running away from home?" Morgan's mom asked.

Morgan grinned. "No, Mom."

"Well, what's with the duffel bag?"

"Just some things I don't really need."

"Like what?" Mom set her newspaper aside and peered curiously at Morgan.

"Just some clothes." Morgan shrugged. "I have a lot of clothes, you know."

"I know. But what are you going to do with those?"

"They're for a friend."

"A friend?"

Morgan sat down on the couch next to Mom now. "I can't really give you all the details. But Emily doesn't really have many clothes right now. I think they moved here in such a hurry that their stuff isn't here yet, you know?"

Mom nodded. "Oh."

"Yeah, and so I thought I could share. I mean, I don't need all the clothes I have, and Emily's been wearing the same jeans every day since she's been here."

Mom smiled. "Morgan, I think that's a great idea. But Emily is a few inches shorter than you. Did you pick out things that will fit?"

"Yeah. In fact, I found some things I'd actually outgrown."

"Is there anything else her family might need?" asked Mom. "You know that Grandma and I would be happy to share."

"I don't know," admitted Morgan. "But I can ask Emily."

"I hope this won't make her feel embarrassed," said Mom.

"I thought about that," admitted Morgan. "I decided that I'm going to tell her it's a God thing. And that God wants his children to share with each other. And so she can't be offended. Unless she wants to get mad at God, that is. And I don't think that's such a good idea."

Mom laughed. "No, I don't think that's such a good idea either. Let me know if we can help."

Morgan put a duffel-bag strap over her shoulder and went outside. She hoped she didn't run into Carlie or Amy just now. She wasn't sure what she would say to them. More than anything, she wanted to respect Emily's privacy. She knew that it had been hard for Emily to open up to her. It might be too much to have Carlie and Amy in on this too.

Morgan glanced both ways, but the neighborhood looked pretty quiet just now. So, shooting up a quick prayer, she darted down the street toward Emily's house. And soon she was knocking at the door.

"It's just me," she called out. "Morgan!"

"Hi, Morgan," said Emily, opening the door. "Come on in."

"Sorry to just pop in unexpectedly again," began Morgan. "I would've called … "

"What's up?" asked Emily. "You moving in or something?"

Morgan laughed. "Not exactly."

"So, what's with the suitcase?"

"Well, I was doing some closet cleaning this afternoon, and I noticed that some of my clothes were getting too small. I think I've grown about three inches this past year. Even my feet got bigger. I used to wear size 6 shoes last fall, and now I'm wearing 8s. I hope they don't keep growing."

"I wear a 6," said Emily.

"Yeah, so I was thinking maybe you could use some of these things." Morgan set the bag on the floor with a thump.

"Really?" Emily stared down at the bag. "You're giving me this?"

"You don't mind, do you?" Morgan braced herself. "I mean, I don't want to offend you, but I was thinking that since we're sisters in the Lord and everything … well, sisters share things, you know."

Emily grinned. "I don't mind at all, Morgan. I'm sick of wearing the same jeans every day." She picked up the bag now. "I can't wait to see what's in here. Want to come into my room while I check it out?"

"Sure." Morgan felt pleased at how easy this was. But when she stepped into Emily's room, she had a shock. Other than an air mattress, some blankets, and a pillow, the place was stark and empty — no personal items, no pictures on the walls, no color.

"Make yourself at home," said Emily sarcastically. "Not much, is it?"

"No … but it's like a blank canvas, Emily. Just think of all we could do with it. Raw potential."

Emily sighed. "Maybe *you* could do something with it, Morgan. But it looks pretty hopeless to me."

"I could definitely do something with it. Will you let me help you fix it up?"

"Really?" Emily's eyes lit up.

"It'd be fun!"

"Hey, knock yourself out." Emily unzipped the bag now, pulling out a pair of khaki pants that were too short for Morgan. "Wow, these are great, Morgan." And just like that, Emily whipped off her jeans and pulled up the khakis. "And they fit too!"

"They look good on you, Emily," said Morgan with excitement. She reached into the bag and pulled out a pale blue T-shirt. "This would look good with them."

The next thing she knew, Emily had on the T-shirt. "How does it look?"

"Fantastic," said Morgan. "The blue is perfect with your eyes."

"I wish I had a mirror," said Emily.

"How about the bathroom?"

So they went into the bathroom, where Emily stretched to see her new hand-me-down outfit in the mirror above the sink.

"Hang on," said Morgan. "I'll be right back."

Then she dashed over to her house where she quickly bagged up some extra hangers for the clothes and then put a full-length mirror under her arm.

"Moving out?" asked Grandma as Morgan walked through the kitchen.

"Mom will explain," she said as she hurried past.

Soon she was back in Emily's room, where Emily proceeded to try on all the clothes, checking them out in the mirror. Morgan hung them one by one on hangers and put them in the closet. Finally they were done, and Emily was back in the khakis and blue T-shirt. She threw her arms around Morgan. "Thank you so much!"

"There's another thing," said Morgan as she reached down to pull a New Testament from a zipper pocket in the bag. "I have several Bibles, and this is a spare. I thought that since you invited Jesus into your heart … well … you might want to start reading it."

"Thank you!" exclaimed Emily. "You're the best friend ever, Morgan."

Morgan could feel herself beaming. "You are too, Emily."

"I don't see how," said Emily. "I mean, here you are giving me things and helping me and taking me to church … I haven't done much of anything to be a good friend."

Morgan laughed. "Hey, you needed me. That's pretty cool."

Emily smiled. "Well, someday I'll repay you — for everything."

Now Morgan looked around Emily's room again. Other than having some colorful items of clothes in her closet, it still looked pretty sad. "So, were you serious about letting me fix up your room?"

"Of course. But I don't want you to feel like you have to, Morgan. You've already done so much."

"Hey, I can't think of anything that'd be more fun, Emily." Morgan glanced at her watch. "It's almost two now. I need to work on some things. Is it okay if I come back in a couple of hours?"

"Fine with me," said Emily. "I'm the only one here anyway."

Morgan grinned. "Okay. See you around four."

"Mom?" called Morgan as soon as she got into the house. "Where are you?"

"In here," called Mom from the laundry room.

"Mom!" exclaimed Morgan. "It was so cool. Emily loved absolutely everything, and she tried it all on and we hung it up in her closet and she told me that I can even fix up her room. I mean, all she has in there is this air mattress and some bedding and I'm going to —"

"Slow down," said Mom, placing a hand on Morgan's shoulder. "And take a breath."

"Sorry, but it's just so exciting. Do you know that it's fun helping others?"

Mom smiled. "It is, isn't it?"

"Anyway, I just remembered that we still have a lot of things in Grandma's storage shed, don't we?"

Mom nodded. "Yes, that had occurred to me too — things from our old apartment that didn't fit in here. And I've been worried that some things will get ruined from the moisture. Do you want to help me go through it?"

"Yeah!"

So Morgan and Mom spent the next couple of hours sorting and sifting through the storage shed. Morgan found pillows and pictures and a lamp and a rug that would cover the stain of Texas just perfectly. They loaded an assortment of items into the car, and by four o'clock they were driving the treasure over to Emily's house.

"This is so beautiful," said Emily as she held a purple and green pillow.

"I'm glad you like it," said Mom. "I'm afraid a lot of our things will be ruined if we leave them in storage much longer. Do you think your mom could use anything? I mean, until your other things arrive?"

Emily glanced at Morgan.

"I told her about how your furniture and things haven't gotten here yet."

Emily nodded. "Yeah, and it could be quite a while before they do."

"Well, if you think your mom wouldn't mind," said Cleo, "I'd love to get some of my things out of the storage unit. I noticed that one of my chairs has been nibbled on by mice."

"You can ask my mom when she gets here in a couple of hours," offered Emily. "I don't think Mom will mind at all." She laughed. "You've seen that we have plenty of room."

Cleo hugged Morgan and said she'd be back in a couple of hours to see what they'd accomplished. Morgan and Emily got to work and in what seemed like no time, the room was transformed. Fabric and pictures decorated the walls. The girls made a sitting area with the rug and some pillows. And a small desk and a bedside table with a lamp helped fill the once-barren room.

Emily and Morgan were sitting on the floor when Morgan's mom returned. "Come and see Emily's room." said Morgan with excitement.

"It's awesome," said Emily as they all three went to look.

"Very nice," said Mom, patting Morgan on the back. "You have a real flare, Morgan. I think you might have to come help out at the shop when school's out. I could use your touch."

"What kind of shop?" asked Emily.

"Didn't I tell you about Mom's shop?" asked Morgan. "It's an import shop. Down by the waterfront. I'll take you there next week. It's really cool."

Just then they heard voices. "Sounds like Mom and Kyle are home," said Emily. "Come and meet them."

"What has happened here?" cried Emily's mom as she stared in shock at Emily's room.

"Mom," said Emily. "I want you to meet my friend Morgan."

"I hope you don't mind," began Morgan's mom, taking one of the bags of groceries from Emily's mother's arms. Emily quickly introduced everyone. Her mom's name was Lisa. And, like Emily, she was a pretty blonde.

"I moved in with my mother a couple of years ago and put a lot of my things in storage," Morgan's mom quickly explained. "Morgan told me how your things haven't arrived yet, and I have furniture and kitchen items just sitting in storage getting damaged by moisture and mice." She looked at Lisa's nervous face. "It would really help me out if I could store my stuff inside a house rather than in a storage shed. You are welcome to it. I mean, until your things arrive, Lisa."

"I don't mind at all," said Lisa. "But it might be a while before our things get here. The … uh … moving van seems to have gotten lost along the way somewhere."

Morgan's mom laughed. "Hey, the longer you can keep these things for me, the happier I'll be."

"Well, thank you." Cleo followed Lisa into the kitchen where they continued to talk.

"This is so cool," said Kyle. "We're going to have real furniture. I can help move it."

"This seems to be working out just fine," Morgan told Emily as they headed back into her bedroom.

Emily looked around her much more colorful room and sighed happily. "It's starting to feel like home here."

Morgan nodded. "You are home, Emily."

"I hope so."

"Remember that feeling I had yesterday?" Morgan reminded her. "How I thought God was working things out for you?"

Emily laughed. "You were totally right!"

chapter ten

Three quiet days passed with no bully attacks and by
Thursday afternoon, Amy questioned whether or not they
really needed to continue their arrangement. She'd made
it clear that she didn't like arriving at school later than
usual. Morgan wished Amy would lighten up. She thought
their walk might be all that was holding the four of them
together.

"Why not stick together?" urged Morgan as she
looked to the others for support. "I mean, we don't know
what those guys are up to right now."

"Besides," added Emily, "we should use this time to
keep working on our plans for fixing up the trailer court."

"That's right," said Carlie. "My dad said to tell you
guys to be ready bright and early on Saturday. He wants to
get back from digging up plants by noon."

"And we need to start some of our fund-raising plans,"
said Amy, finally getting into the spirit of things. "I've
already started collecting cans. Man, you should see how
much pop my sisters and brother drink. You'd think their
teeth would be rotten by now."

"And my dad told me that he'd help us make some planters out of the old fence pieces that we piled up last weekend," said Carlie. "So that'll be free."

"Cool," said Morgan. "And my grandma read something in the paper about how the dump is giving away recycled mulch."

"Recycled mulch?" said Amy. "Like, what is that supposed to be?"

Morgan shrugged. "I don't know, but it's free, and Grandma said it would come in handy." She turned to Carlie. "Do you think your dad could get some for us in his pickup?"

Carlie nodded. "And your grandma's right. It will come in handy."

Morgan lowered her voice and hissed through her teeth, "Don't look now, but I think we're being watched. Up there by the fence next to that alley ... I see a bike tire."

"Oh, brother," said Carlie. "They just don't give up, do they?"

"Let's just act natural," said Morgan. "Don't let them think they're getting to us."

"I'm getting out my phone." Amy paused to dig in her backpack.

"That's not a bad idea," said Morgan as they waited for her.

"Yeah, it might show them that we're not going to take it anymore," said Emily.

So the girls continued walking, with Morgan and Carlie in the lead and Emily and Amy following. Sure enough, there was Derrick. He was with a boy that Morgan didn't recognize, and both of them were scowling, trying to look tough.

"Don't act scared," whispered Morgan as they got closer. "Show 'em your cool face."

The four girls continued walking, and Morgan made an attempt at light conversation. "Nice weather we're having, isn't it?"

"Yeah," said Carlie. "And only a week until summer va — "

"Thought I told you trailer trash to stay off our turf," snarled Derrick, pulling out his bike to block their way.

"I thought we told you this was a public street," said Morgan, still walking.

"Public for some people," said the other boy with narrowed eyes. He was taller than Derrick with a buzz cut and a bad complexion. "Not for people like you."

Morgan and Carlie were only a foot or so away from the boys, and Amy and Emily were right behind them. Morgan's eyes fell to a piece of wood Derrick brandished in his hand. She felt a tightening in her chest and throat. Her eyes widened slightly and she prayed a quick prayer. Then she took a deep breath and pointed calmly at the stick. "What are you planning on doing, Derrick? You think you're going to club us with that?"

He swung the stick and grinned. "Just protecting my territory."

"I'm calling the police," said Amy as she pushed a button on her phone and held it to her ear.

"That's a good idea," said Morgan. "We have four witnesses and—"

"I'm outta here," said the buzz-cut boy, taking off down the alley on his bike.

Morgan looked directly at Derrick now. "What about you?" she asked. "Want to stick around for when the police arrive, or should we just tell them where to find you?"

"This is Amy Ngo," Amy said in her know-it-all voice. Then Amy very accurately described their location. "We're being harassed by some older boys and one of them is armed with—"

"Hey, take it easy," said Derrick quickly. "We were just fooling around. You don't have to take it so seriously."

"Seriously?" Morgan stepped a little closer now. "You knocked Emily off her bike and ruined her front tire. Is that not serious?"

"We were just messing around with her."

"You hurt her!" shouted Carlie with her hands on her hips. "And you've threatened all of us. And we are sick and tired of it, Derrick Smith. And we are going to tell the police—"

"Look, I'm sorry," he said quickly, and Morgan could tell that he really was scared now. "I'll fix the bike too. Just don't tell, okay?"

Morgan turned and looked at the other girls, and Amy winked at her. "Hold on a minute," Amy said into the phone, then to Morgan, "I guess we could give him one last chance."

Morgan turned back to face Derrick. "Okay, we're going to give you one chance, but if you do anything like this again — to anyone — we will definitely report you."

"That's right," said Carlie.

"And you have to replace Emily's bent bike wheel," said Morgan. She glanced at Derrick's bike now. "I think it's the same size as your bike tire. Maybe you'd like to hand that over to us right now, Mr. Smith?"

Derrick looked flustered now. "But how will I get home?"

"The same way Emily got home," said Carlie. "You'll walk. But at least you won't be limping."

"Hand over the tire," said Morgan in a firm voice.

"Yes, I'm still on the line," said Amy into the phone. "Yes, sir, we're still trying to determine whether or not this boy really intends to hurt us. Yes, he's still here. Yes, he still has the club in his hand."

Derrick tossed the board aside and hopped off his bike. In the same instant he snapped the quick-release gadgets on his front tire. Then he rolled it over to Emily. "Here."

She just nodded. Then Derrick took off on foot down the alley, awkwardly wheeling his disabled bike beside him as he went. The girls stood and watched until he turned the corner at the end of the alley, then they all clapped and cheered, giving one another high fives to celebrate their victory.

"Way to go, Morgan!" said Carlie, slapping her on the back.

"Way to go, Amy!" said Morgan. Then she thought of something. "But what about the police, Amy? Won't they come anyway?"

"Yeah," said Emily nervously. "I ... uh ... I heard that if you call 9-1-1, the police will come no matter what." She peered down the street, looking as if she was about to run. Morgan suddenly realized what Emily was doing. She knew that Emily couldn't give her name to the police because it might lead her dad there.

Amy just laughed. "No fear; I punched in the numerals, but I never hit *Send*. I figured we should just scare the boys to start with. If they didn't respond, I would've put the call through — just like that." She snapped her fingers.

Morgan saw Emily relax and step back toward the girls.

"Maybe we should've done that before," admitted Carlie.

"Maybe …, " said Amy with a sly smile. "But then we never would've become friends."

Morgan stared at Amy. "So, you really do consider us your friends?"

Amy looked surprised. "Of course. Aren't you?"

Morgan nodded. "Sure." Then she looked at the other two. "Right?"

"Right," said Carlie.

"Right," echoed Emily.

Then Morgan put out her right hand, and the other three girls put their hands on top of it. "All for one," said Morgan. And the other three joined in with, "and one for all!"

"Does that make us the Four Musketeers?" asked Emily as they walked toward home.

Morgan laughed. "Yeah. Something like that."

"Anyone want to join in me in soliciting returnable pop cans from the neighborhood today?" asked Amy.

"Soliciting?" said Carlie. "What's that mean?"

"Begging," said Morgan.

So it was agreed the four girls would "solicit" their neighborhood for cans for the next two afternoons. But it didn't take long before it turned into something of a competition. Thinking it was safer to go out as teams of two, it was soon Morgan and Emily against Carlie and Amy. And, driven to outdo each other, both teams ended up going outside the mobile-home park as well.

By Saturday, both teams had gathered an impressive collection of soda cans. At six in the morning, they loaded numerous large garbage bags into Carlie's dad's pickup, since he'd agreed to drop them by the store to cash them in before heading out to the woods. Amy had tied her and Carlie's bags with pieces of bright red yarn. "Just so we can tell them apart," she explained as they climbed into Mr. Garcia's club-cab pickup.

"I think the winners should get a prize," said Morgan, certain that she and Emily had outdone them.

"Yes," said Amy. "I agree. Maybe the losers should buy lunch."

"But then we'd have to use some of our money," pointed out Carlie. "And that would mean less flowers and paint and things."

"Oh, right," Amy agreed.

"How about if the losers fix lunch," suggested Morgan.

"You're on," said Amy.

Mr. Garcia just chuckled as he dropped the girls at Safeway. Then each pair of girls took a turn at the recycling machine, carefully loading their cans one by one until it was time to print out the receipt for cash.

"Twenty-four dollars and fifty-five cents," announced Morgan, feeling a little dismayed. "I thought it would be more than that," she admitted. "That was a lot of cans."

"Twenty-nine dollars and thirty-five cents," proclaimed Amy. "We win!"

"Wow," said Carlie, "that's more than fifty bucks."

"That's exactly fifty-three dollars and ninety cents," said Amy.

"She's the queen of mental math," Morgan told Emily.

"Well, congratulations to Amy and Carlie," said Emily.

"Looks like we'll be fixing lunch today." Morgan winked at Emily. Then as Carlie and Amy were at the register collecting their cash, Morgan told her that she'd already warned her grandma that the girls would be hungry for a big lunch today. "She's got it all under control."

Emily grinned. "Sounds like we'll be eating in style."

By noon the girls had dug up dozens of small trees and shrubs. Mr. Garcia had gotten permits in all the girls' names, and each one of them filled her quota. Fortunately, because of Carlie and her dad, it looked like most of the plants might survive too.

"It looks like a mini-forest," said Carlie as her dad closed the tailgate.

"Just think how great these are going to look planted all around the trailer court," said Amy.

"But you'll need to get them planted as quickly as possible," Mr. Garcia warned them as he began driving down the forest-service road toward town. "You don't want their roots to get dry."

Amy sighed as she held up her filthy hands. "This is turning out to be pretty hard work."

"But it'll be worth it," Carlie reminded her. "When you see how much better everything looks."

"I hope so," said Amy. "My fingernails are ruined."

"That's why you should use gloves," Carlie pointed out.

"What's for lunch?" asked Amy, staring at Morgan and Emily. "I'm starved."

"Me too," said Carlie, grinning. "And it better be good."

"You have your cell phone on you?" Morgan asked Amy.

"Yeah, why?"

"If you let me call home, I can find out about lunch."

As it turned out, Morgan's grandma had already cleaned up their barbecue grill and had hamburger patties and potato salad ready to go.

"And brownies and ice cream for dessert," Morgan added to finish describing the menu to her friends.

"Woo-hoo!" cheered Carlie. "Hurry up, Dad!"

Morgan figured it was a good thing that she and Emily had lost the can contest. She doubted that any of the other girls could've pulled together a lunch like her grandma. And as the long, hard day wore on, and the digging and planting continued, Morgan's grandma continued to provide the girls with snacks and drinks.

"You four are amazing," said Grandma as she looked at the fully planted landscape strip at the front of the trailer park.

"And just wait until we add flowers," said Carlie. "It will be even prettier then."

"And you should see the planters that her dad's making out of some old wood," said Amy. "They'll go over there."

"And we still have some painting to do," Emily pointed out.

"And my dad's making a letter $\mathcal{V}$ to replace the one that's missing from the sign," said Carlie.

"No more Harbor *eeuw*," said Morgan. And they all laughed.

But as hard as the girls worked all day, they knew they had a long way to go yet. And even though the next day was Sunday, Morgan's mom told her it was okay to continue the work. "But *after* church."

"No problem," agreed Morgan. "I already promised Emily that we'd take her with us again."

So on Sunday afternoon, after church, Carlie talked her aunt into driving the girls over to a nursery where all the flowers were on sale. "Tia Maria is kind of a flower expert," explained Carlie as they drove across town. "She can help us to pick the right ones for the right places."

"Why don't we just pick the ones that are prettiest?" asked Amy.

"Because some flowers like to grow in the shade," said Carlie. "And some like the full sun."

"And there's a lot of full sun out in front," said Emily.

"We need to get some paint too," said Morgan. "For the sign."

"But nothing too wild," warned Amy. "No garish colors, Morgan."

Morgan frowned. "Are you suggesting that I'd pick out garish colors? *Moi?*"

"Well, I've *seen* your room."

Morgan pretended to be offended. "Well, I've seen your room too, Amy. And I wouldn't just naturally assume that you'd want to paint the sign *lavender*. And you can be sure I don't want to paint it something weird either. Actually, I was thinking of Harbor colors. Maybe tan and light blue; you know, like the sand and sea."

"Oh, that sounds pretty," said Emily.

By the end of the day, Harbor View looked totally transformed. After dinner, the neighbors began coming out of their homes and commenting on the improvements. But the girls didn't see any sign of Mr. Greeley. And Morgan was starting to feel nervous. *What if he didn't approve of something? What if he's mad that we repainted the sign?*

"It makes me want to spruce up my own yard," admitted old Mrs. Hardwick as she stood by the entrance and surveyed their work. "If it wasn't for my arthritis, that is.

Maybe I should hire you girls to help me out."

"I'd love to help," said Carlie. "I plan on being a real landscaper some day."

"Looks like you're off to a good start," said Mrs. Hardwick. "You girls worked wonders with this place. And to think you did this all on your own. It's really amazing."

"Oh, we had a little help," admitted Morgan.

"That gives me an idea," said Mrs. Hardwick. "My son works at the *Boscoe Bay News*. I think I'll give him a call. He might like to come out here to get this as a human-interest story."

"Really?" said Amy, smoothing her hair as if she thought she might be photographed. "Do you think he'd come?"

"Don't know why not."

The girls were just sweeping mulch from the street and watering the plants when Gary Hardwick pulled up and handed them his card. "I'm with the *Boscoe Bay News*," he said, "and I hear you girls are regular little miracle workers."

Morgan laughed. "God's the only miracle worker I know."

"We're just *hard* workers," said Amy. "And I have the blisters to prove it."

So Gary took some photos and asked some questions and told the girls to watch out for Tuesday's paper. The local paper was so small it only came out on Tuesdays and Saturdays.

Finally the girls called it a day. Morgan took a long, hot shower and tumbled into bed, so tired she didn't know how she'd ever wake up in time to walk with her friends to school. Still, she didn't want to make Amy mad at her.

chapter eleven

"Has anyone seen Mr. Greeley around?" asked Morgan as the four girls walked to school together on Monday.

"I think he's hiding out," said Amy. "My parents said he's probably worried that we're going to send him a bill."

Morgan laughed. "Yeah, right."

"I wonder if he likes it," said Emily.

"How could he not like it?" asked Carlie. "It looks fantastic. Everyone is saying so."

"Yeah, but he's such a grump," pointed out Morgan. "Maybe he likes for things to be ugly."

"Kind of like Oscar the Grouch?" said Amy.

"Exactly." Morgan laughed. "Greeley the Grouch." Of course, as soon as she said it, she felt a little guilty.

"What would we do if he didn't like it?" asked Carlie nervously. "Do you think he could make us undo what we've done?"

"Maybe," admitted Amy. "I mean, if he's really the owner. My parents said that they're pretty sure he is. So, I guess he can do whatever he likes with Harbor View."

"Well, I wish he'd come out and show his face and thank us," said Morgan.

But two days passed and none of the girls saw Mr. Greeley. Even when the article and the photo of the girls standing at the entrance of the park came out in Tuesday's paper, Mr. Greeley was nowhere to be seen.

"Do you think he took a trip?" asked Morgan as the four girls sat at her table looking at the newspaper.

"Maybe he died," said Emily in a spooky voice.

"Died?" Carlie frowned at her.

"Yeah," continued Emily, getting even more dramatic. "He could be over there right now, lying on his floor, dead!"

"Stop it," said Amy. "You're creeping me out."

"Just kidding," said Emily, tossing a sly grin at Morgan.

"Oh, he's probably just lying low," said Morgan. "He has to be embarrassed that it took us four girls to get this place back into shape."

"Yeah, I bet he's ashamed that he didn't do something like this way sooner," said Carlie. "Do you think he'll even help us to keep it up?"

"That's a good question," said Amy. "I don't want to spend my whole summer on a yard crew."

"We could take turns," suggested Carlie. "I don't mind doing it."

"Yeah," said Amy sarcastically. "We could take turns and then we could send Mr. Greeley the big fat bill!"

A couple more days passed without a word from Mr. Greeley, and Morgan was actually beginning to think that

Emily could be right. What if Mr. Greeley really was dead? Wouldn't she feel terrible for calling him *Greeley the Grouch?*

On Thursday night, before going to sleep, she decided she should be praying for Mr. Greeley. In fact, she was surprised this hadn't occurred to her sooner. *The poor old guy probably doesn't have anyone who cares enough to pray for him.* And tomorrow she would tell Emily about her plan and see if she wanted to pray for him too. More than ever, she hoped the old man wasn't dead!

Morgan wasn't sure what made her get up so early on Friday morning. Maybe it was because this was the last day of school and she was excited to see summer vacation officially begin. Or maybe she just sensed that something was up. But as she stood at the kitchen sink, looking out the window that overlooked the entrance to the mobile-home court, she suddenly felt sick.

"*Mom!*" she screamed. "*Grandma!*"

"What is it?" said Mom as she ran into the kitchen half dressed.

"What on earth?" cried Grandma. "Are you hurt?"

Morgan stood in front of the window, pointing. "*Look!*" Mom leaned over. "Oh, my!"

"Oh, dear," said Grandma sadly.

Plants were pulled out by their roots. Trash was thrown all over the place. Even the recently painted sign had been vandalized, with red paint splattered like blood across it.

"Who would do this?" said Morgan, tears of anger streaming down her cheeks.

Grandma put her arm around her shoulders. "I don't know, dear. But whoever did this must be very disturbed."

"And mean," said Mom. "I'm so sorry, Morgan. After all your hard work … "

"I'm going out to see how bad it is," said Morgan.

"I'm calling the police," said Mom.

"I'm going to pray," said Grandma.

It looked even worse when Morgan got outside. Plants that they'd worked so hard to dig up and transplant looked like slain soldiers on the battlefield now, scattered all over the ground, wounded and dying.

"What happened?" cried Carlie, coming over to join her.

"Someone is crazy," said Morgan, sadly picking up a small pine tree.

"Why?" said Carlie, sobbing loudly as she picked up a smashed marigold plant. "Why would someone do this? Why would they hurt these poor innocent plants?"

"And us."

Soon Amy and Emily were out. All four walked around, surveying the damage and grieving as they attempted to salvage what they could before it was time to go to school. A patrol car arrived just before eight, and

Morgan's mom spoke to the police officers, giving out as much information as they had. And that was practically nothing.

"You girls are going to be late for school," Mom called out. "You better get going."

"Do we have to?" asked Morgan. "Who will clean this up?"

"It's your last day," said Mom. "You're supposed to go and have fun."

"Yeah, right," said Morgan in a grumpy voice.

"Let's go," said Amy. "We might not be tardy if we hurry."

"Who cares?" said Morgan. "It's the last day anyway."

"I have a perfect attendance record," admitted Amy. "And as upsetting as this stupid vandalism is, I don't intend to blow it now."

"I usually love the last day of school," said Morgan as the four girls walked as fast as they could toward school. "Now, I don't even care."

"It's a waste of time," said Amy.

"Why?" asked Carlie.

"Because you know we won't do any schoolwork. We'll just play silly games and stuff. I think they should just cancel the last day of school altogether."

"How would you do that?" asked Emily. "No matter what you called it — or even if you did it a day early — there'd still have to be a *last* day."

"But it could just be a regular day," insisted Amy.

They argued back and forth about this as they hurried to school. And Amy's perfect record remained as they got into the classroom just before the bell rang.

It turned out to be an okay day, but only because of all the fun and games, which would have been more fun under other circumstances. Still, Morgan was glad when it was over. And as she gathered up all her junk and loaded it into her backpack, she began to think about what they were about to go home to, and suddenly she felt like crying.

"Are you sad to be leaving sixth grade, Morgan?" asked Miss Thurman with concerned eyes.

"Hmm?" Morgan stared up at her. "Yeah, I mean, I guess so."

"Well, you're going to do just fine in seventh grade," her teacher assured her. "Just make sure you do your homework and don't get behind."

Morgan forced a smile. "Yeah. I'll try to remember that."

Soon all the good-byes and good lucks had been said, and the four girls were trudging back toward home again.

"I'm so bummed," said Morgan when they were about halfway there.

"Me too," said Carlie. "I feel like someone has died."

"Who do you think did it?" asked Amy. "Who could be that mean? That heartless?"

"Mr. Greeley is pretty mean," said Emily.

"You don't think he'd do something like that, do you?" said Carlie. "I mean, especially if he owns the place. It doesn't make sense."

"But what if ... " Emily seemed to be noodling on something. "What if he had a reason for keeping the place looking run-down?"

"A reason?" said Carlie. "What could that be?"

"Maybe tax evasion," suggested Amy. "My parents are always complaining about taxes. But they say that tax cheaters do time."

"Or maybe Mr. Greeley wants the trailer court to get so run down that everyone leaves," said Emily.

"Why?"

"Maybe he wants to redevelop it like Boscoe Bay Resort," said Emily. "My mom works there, and she told me there was some big land scandal about that place."

"That's right," remembered Morgan. "They had this big land-use war. It was in the news all the time. But finally the developers won."

"Yeah," said Amy. "My parents were against it too. They were worried that the resort's restaurant would take business away from their restaurant."

"Did it?"

She shrugged. "I don't know. I don't think so."

"Do you guys really think Mr. Greeley could've done something like this?" asked Morgan. "It just seems so weird."

"Well, he is pretty weird," said Emily.

"And he sure has been staying out of sight."

"Yeah," agreed Emily. "He wasn't even around this morning. You'd think he'd at least have come out to talk to the police."

"Yeah," said Amy. "That's pretty suspicious."

Now they were almost home, and Morgan's stomach began to feel slightly sick as she prepared herself to witness the damage all over again. But as the entrance to Harbor View came into sight, she noticed that several people from the neighborhood seemed to be milling around. And as they got closer, it became apparent that these people had shovels and wheelbarrows and they seemed to be working.

"Look!" shouted Carlie, starting to jog toward the trailer court. "They're fixing it back up for us!"

Sure enough, members of the girls' own families, along with other neighbors, were out doing various chores. And the work that the girls had done during the past weekend appeared to be in the process of being restored.

"How did this happen?" Morgan asked her grandma. She was sitting in a lawn chair, and she had a tub filled with ice and cold drinks that she was sharing with the workers.

"Word of the vandalism traveled fast," she began. "People started coming out and asking if they could help. And the next thing we knew, we had a regular work crew going here."

"It really wasn't that much work," said Carlie's aunt as she patted down the dirt around a juniper plant. "You girls did the hard stuff in the first place. We're just putting things back where they belong now."

"Were very many plants dead?" asked Carlie with wide, concerned eyes.

"Time will tell, *mija*," said her aunt. "But it's worth trying, eh?"

"Definitely!" said Carlie. "Let me dump my stuff from school, and I'll be back out to help too."

"I still have paint for the sign," said Morgan. "I'll bet after a couple of coats, that red gunk will be history."

Everyone worked hard, and just as the group was talking about quitting, a bright red and yellow pizza van pulled into the trailer court. Morgan looked up from painting a third coat on the vandalized sign.

"I have a bunch of pizzas to deliver," a young man hollered at her. "Where do you want me to put them?"

She looked over at him. "I don't know." She glanced over at Grandma. "Did you order pizza?"

Grandma shook her head. "Not me, honey."

"Did *anyone* order pizza?" yelled Morgan, hoping that someone would step up and take responsibility. But everyone just shrugged and looked around.

"The man who called already paid for it," said the young man. "He said to give the pizzas to the workers here." He smiled at Morgan. "Would that be you guys?"

Morgan grinned. "Yeah, I guess so."

So the guy went back to his pizza van and emerged with a stack of giant pizza boxes. "Come and get it!" he yelled.

Morgan took a couple of the pizzas from him and whispered, "Did the man tell you his name?"

"He told me not to tell."

She made a disappointed face.

"But he sounded like an old dude," he said in a quiet voice.

"Oh." She nodded. "Thanks."

Before long the pizza van was gone, and everyone was gathered in Grandma's yard. "You run into the house and fetch some paper plates and napkins," she told Morgan. And soon they were all pigging out on pizza, laughing and joking. And for the first time since Morgan had lived here, she was actually getting to know a bunch of her neighbors.

"I called my son again today," said Mrs. Hardwick. "He was by this morning taking pictures of the vandalism. It might even make it into tomorrow's paper. Shame on whoever did it."

"I heard voices last night," said a retired man named Mr. Ramsay. Morgan had just met him today, and he seemed pretty nice. He lived in the mobile home just across from Grandma's. "Sounded like kids to me," he continued.

"I told the police." He shook his head. "Wish I'd gone out to check on it. But I didn't think it was anything serious at the time."

"Maybe we need a neighborhood watch," said a young mom named Leanne. "I remember last summer when some houses got broken into. It was kind of scary." And soon all the adults were discussing the best ways to start up something like that.

"Are you thinking what I'm thinking?" Amy said to Morgan as the four girls gathered together off to the side.

"About last night's vandals?" asked Morgan.

"Do you think it was Derrick and his buddies?" said Emily.

Amy and Morgan both nodded.

"I'd like to murder them!" said Carlie in a seething tone.

"Carlie!" said Morgan.

"Okay, not murder them. But I'd like them to suffer."

"We don't know for sure that it was them," said Morgan.

"You don't still think it was Mr. Greeley, do you?" asked Amy.

"Well, no ... " Morgan considered telling them about what the pizza guy had said about an old man ordering the pizzas. But she wasn't sure that meant it was Mr. Greeley.

"I think it was Derrick," said Amy. "The question is, did he have help?"

"Mr. Ramsay said 'voices,'" pointed out Emily.

"And I'm sure Derrick was furious at us for making him give Emily his bike wheel," said Morgan.

"And for being humiliated like that," added Carlie.

"It makes sense," said Amy. "But what are we going to do?"

Morgan glanced back over to where Mr. Ramsay seemed to be heading the beginning of a real neighborhood-watch group. "Maybe we won't have to do anything," she said, nodding at the adults. "Maybe they'll take care of it."

"Cool," said Carlie. "Then we can all sleep better at night."

"Hello," called a voice from across the street. Suddenly the crowd of people sitting around Grandma's yard got quiet as Mr. Greeley slowly walked toward them. "Don't want to bust up your party," he said in a gruff voice. "But there are some girls I need to have a word with." He scowled at the group. "I think they know who they are."

"If you're talking about our hardworking young ladies," began Mr. Ramsay, quickly getting to his feet. "You may need to — "

"Don't worry," barked Mr. Greeley. "I'm not going to hurt them."

"But what do you — "

"I just want a word with them!" Mr. Greeley folded his arms across his chest. "If you don't mind."

"It's okay," said Morgan, quickly going over to where the old man was standing. "You want to talk to us, sir?"

"That's right. All four of you. March yourselves over to my place, right now."

The other three girls looked terrified, as if they expected Mr. Greeley to eat them for dinner or something. "It's okay," Morgan assured them. Then, under her breath, "There are *four* of us and only one of him."

The crowd watched quietly as the four girls followed Mr. Greeley across the street to his mobile home. Morgan hesitated, looked at her friends, and then followed Mr. Greeley up the porch steps and into his house. To her relief, her friends came too. Still, her knees were shaking as she stood there in his living room that doubled as the office for Harbor View. What could he possibly want with them anyway? Surely, he didn't think they were responsible for last night's vandalism. Why would they destroy their own work?

chapter twelve

"I know what you girls did," Mr. Greeley spoke in a serious voice. "Although I'm not quite sure why you did it." He slowly shook his head. "And, to be honest, I didn't think you had it in you. But you did." Now he actually smiled at them. "And I just wanted to say thank you."

Morgan sighed with relief. "You're very welcome, Mr. Greeley."

"Now, will you all tell me your names?" he asked.

So, one by one, they introduced themselves to him and he shook each of their hands, personally thanking each of them.

"Pleasure to meet you, ladies." He reached into his pocket now. "And I have something that I want to give you. As a token of my gratitude." He pulled out a key. "It might not be anything you want or can use ... or maybe it will." His brow creased. "But I have a feeling that girls like you will know what to do with it."

He looked at Morgan. "You seem to be the leader of the pack, Morgan. Here." He put the key in her hand.

"But what's it go to?" she asked.

He peered out at the sky that was just starting to get dusky. "Well, it's getting late tonight. Maybe I'd best show you girls tomorrow. That all right by you?"

"Sure," she said. "Of course."

"You come over here around nine, and I'll show you what the key goes to."

She thanked him, as did the others, although none of them had a clue as to why.

"And I wanted you to know that I was real disappointed when I came out this morning and saw what the vandals done to the place. I would've liked to have wrung some necks." He sighed loudly. "But then when I seen the residents here all coming out to help put things back to order … well, it was enough to give an old man like me some hope. Thank you, ladies."

They thanked him again and promised to be back at nine in the morning, and then they left.

"That was so weird," said Amy as they were crossing the street.

"But sweet," said Morgan as they paused near the area where the adults were earnestly discussing neighborhood security. "Mr. Greeley is really a sweet old guy."

"But kinda scary," said Carlie. "I mean, I saw this movie once, and the old guy acted really nice, but in the end he killed everyone."

"Your parents let you watch that?" asked Morgan.

"It was at my cousins' house."

"Well, I agree with Morgan," said Emily. "I think Mr. Greeley is a nice old guy. Just lonely."

"You know what else," said Morgan.

"What?" they all asked.

"I think Mr. Greeley bought the pizzas."

"Why didn't he tell anyone?" asked Amy.

"Maybe he wants to be a mystery man," said Emily.

"Well, he's definitely mysterious," admitted Carlie.

"I wonder what the key is for," said Morgan as she fingered the key that was safely tucked into her pocket.

"Maybe it's to a secret vault," said Amy, "full of money."

"Yeah, right." Morgan rolled her eyes. "Like Mr. Greeley is rich."

"He might've robbed a bank," said Amy.

"Maybe it's to a car," said Carlie. "A brand-new Corvette."

"Like, what would we do with a car?" asked Morgan. "We can't even drive."

"Maybe it's to a house," said Emily. "A nice little beach house that we can use this summer."

"You wish," said Amy. "Why would someone like Greeley have a nice beach house?"

"I can dream," said Emily.

"Maybe …," said Morgan dramatically, "it's the key to his heart."

Amy gave her a playful shove. "Man, you're really getting goofy over the old geezer, aren't you?"

"Well, I think he wants to be our friend," she said defensively.

"And maybe we'll have to wait until tomorrow to find out what the key is for," said Emily.

"Why don't we meet at my house," said Morgan. "Nine o'clock sharp."

It was dark out now. Families had started to regroup, and people were heading for home. Morgan and her mom picked up a few stray pieces of trash and started back into the house.

"Do you think I should stay up and watch for vandals?" asked Morgan once they were on the porch.

"No," said Mom. "Don't worry about that. Mr. Ramsay has it all under control. You girls have done quite enough for the neighborhood. At least for the time being." She put her arm around Morgan's shoulders. "Hey, what did Mr. Greeley say to you girls?"

So Morgan told her about the key.

"A key?"

"Yeah. We don't have the slightest idea why. But he's going to show us in the morning."

"Sounds exciting," said Mom. "Just make sure that it's something safe, Morgan. I wouldn't like to hear about you four girls riding around on a motorcycle or anything dangerous like that." Mom's eyes sparkled.

She laughed. "Don't worry, Mom."

Morgan got up with the sun the next morning. She knew it was crazy since it wasn't even a school day. In fact, it was the first official day of summer vacation. But she was thinking about the key sitting on her dresser — and something else — Morgan hurried to the kitchen window. What if the vandals had struck again?

To her huge relief everything looked perfectly fine. In fact she even noticed Mr. Greeley outside dragging a hose behind him. It looked like he'd been watering their plants.

Finally, after what seemed like days, it was 8:45, and Morgan went out on the porch to wait for her friends to show up. At nine o'clock sharp all three of them arrived, and the four of them marched across the street like they were on a mission.

"What if this is just a trick?" said Amy as they paused in front of Mr. Greeley's house.

"A trick?" Morgan frowned. "Why would he want to trick us?"

"Because he's really a mean guy who's just trying to act nice?" said Carlie.

"Because he's really going to murder us?" said Amy.

"*You guys!*" Morgan turned and glared at her friends. "If you don't want to come, you don't have to. But I intend to find out what this key goes to." She went onto the porch and knocked on the door.

Mr. Greeley emerged wearing his dusty old ball cap and a serious expression. "You ready?"

"Yep," said Morgan.

"Follow me."

So, feeling like she'd just joined boot camp, Morgan followed Mr. Greeley with her three friends trailing behind her. She had no idea where they were going, but he seemed to be heading toward the trail that led down to the dunes and then to the beach. The girls hoped that Amy and Carlie's foul-play suspicions were wrong.

Then, instead of continuing down the beach trail, he turned sharply to the right, where a newly cut path — one that she had never seen before — led into the tall beach grass that grew thick in the dunes. The area Grandma had warned her not to explore, since "you could get lost for days out there."

"Uh, where are we going?" she asked in a nervous voice, glancing over her shoulder to be certain her friends were still behind her. They were there, but they looked as worried as she felt. What could possibly be back here anyway?

Then he turned another sharp corner to the left and suddenly, right in front of them was something Morgan had never seen before. It was a big bus! It looked like a school bus except that it had been painted in a wild array of colors. And although the paint had faded some, probably from the coastal weather, it was still very bright. And kind of pretty too.

"A hippie bus?" said Amy, stepping next to Morgan.

Mr. Greeley cleared his throat. "I could be all wrong," he told them, "but I got to thinking this might make for a good clubhouse. You know, for you girls to fix up and play in and stuff. But maybe I'm just all wet ... I mean, what do I know about what girls like to do?"

"Can we look inside?" Morgan asked eagerly.

"Sure," he said. "That's what the key is for."

So Morgan unlocked the door and they all went inside.

"This is cool," said Morgan as she looked at the little wooden table and benches that were attached to the wall.

"It needs some cleaning and fixing up," he admitted. "But then you girls seem pretty good at that sort of thing."

"I think it's absolutely wonderful," said Morgan, grinning at him. "I think it's a great clubhouse."

"So do I," said Emily. "Thank you so much, Mr. Greeley!"

"Was this your bus?" asked Morgan.

"Oh, in a way it was ... but it's yours now."

"It's like a playhouse," said Carlie as she opened one of the built-in cupboards above the table.

"It is kind of cool," admitted Amy as she examined an empty closet. "Someone must've put a lot of work into making this."

"Well, it's all yours now," he said, bowing slightly as he backed out the door. "And I'll leave you ladies to it. Enjoy!"

They all thanked him and watched as he walked away.

"Wow," said Morgan. "Our very own bus."

"It needs a good cleaning," said Carlie as she pulled down a spider's web.

"And some new curtains," said Morgan as she fingered the faded fabric. "But I can take care of that."

"It could be our clubhouse," said Emily. "If we wanted to have a club, that is."

"Aren't clubs for little kids?" said Amy with a frown. "Baby stuff?"

"That depends," said Morgan. "Lots of grown-ups have clubs. And I, for one, would love having a place like this — fixed up, I mean — where I could hang out with my friends and listen to music and talk and do art and all kinds of stuff. Wouldn't you guys?"

Of course, they all agreed. Why shouldn't they agree? The place was loaded with potential — and it was all theirs!

"Let's make a list," said Amy as she found a pencil and an old spiral notebook with yellowed pages.

"What for?" asked Emily.

"For all the things we want to fix up."

"Here we go again," said Carlie, rolling her eyes. "Making lists … fixing things up …"

"Yeah," said Morgan with a big grin. "Isn't it great?"

Soon they each had a list of their own. Carlie was going to bring some cleaning things from her house. Amy had some dishes left over from the restaurant that she wanted to donate. "In case we decide to eat here some time." Morgan and Emily were off to look for curtain fabric and some other items to make the bus more livable — and fun! But before they left, they all just stood outside and looked up at it in amazement.

"Can you believe this is *really* ours?" said Morgan. "To do with as we please?"

"Yeah, it's pretty cool," admitted Amy. "Our very own bus."

"It looks like a rainbow," observed Emily. "The colors, you know."

"Like our own personal rainbow," said Carlie.

"Just like a promise," said Morgan.

"Huh?" asked Emily. "How's that?"

"The rainbow," said Morgan. "It's God's promise."

"For what?" asked Carlie.

"For us," said Morgan.

"But what's the promise *for*?" demanded Amy.

Morgan smiled. "I think it's a promise for friendship."

So it was agreed, their new clubhouse would be called the Rainbow Bus. Of course, they would keep their personal rainbow top secret. Well, except for their parents.

They knew they would have to let them in on it. But other than that, this secret belonged to the four of them — their Rainbow Bus — a promise that their friendship would continue. At least until the end of summer, Morgan hoped. Because who knew what would happen when fall came and they all started seventh grade? But right now — with their very own bus, good friends, and the first day of vacation — it looked as if this might be the best summer ever!

Mystery Bus

chapter one

"I'm not sure which is worse," said Amy holding her nose. "That old musty smell before we started cleaning up in here or Carlie's Lysol. Pee-euw!"

"You want it clean, don't you?" said Carlie, waving her spray bottle of disinfectant in Amy's face.

"Clean, but not stinky."

"Look, this is the way my mom does it in our house," said Carlie, pushing a long, dark curl away from her face. "Are you saying our house is stinky?"

"I'm saying that—"

"Stop arguing!" yelled Morgan as she laced an orange and red striped curtain over a metal rod. "And instead of complaining about everything, Amy, why don't you just open a window and let some fresh air in here?"

"Wow," said Carlie, pausing from her scrubbing long enough to stare at the curtain in Morgan's hands. "That's really bright."

"So, are you the one complaining now?" asked Morgan as she held the curtain up to the window to see how it looked.

"I think it's pretty," said Emily. The fabric reminded her of a sunset. That's what she'd told Morgan when they picked it out of the big box of remnant fabrics. Morgan's grandma said they could use whatever they liked for the bus. "I thought I might make a crazy quilt someday," she'd told them. "But you girls could make that funny old bus into a crazy quilt too."

The girls' families had all been over to see the old bus on the first day that Mr. Greeley had presented it to them as a thank-you gift for cleaning up the trailer park. Mr. Greeley was the owner of the Harbor View Mobile-Home Court. At that time, the bus had been pretty messy with cobwebs and mouse droppings and dust and grime. The girls had been working hard since then, and the results were beginning to show.

"I wasn't complaining about the fabric," Carlie said defensively. "I just thought it was kinda bright is all. That a crime now or something?"

It was their third day of cleaning up the Rainbow Bus, and for some reason tempers seemed to be running a little warm this morning. Emily figured it could be due to the weather.

"Can you believe how hot it's getting already?" she said, hoping to change the subject. "My mom said it's supposed to get up to like ninety-six degrees this afternoon."

"I've lived in Boscoe Bay my whole life," said Amy. She pushed her straight, black bangs away from her forehead and flopped onto the narrow couch, "and I don't remember it ever getting this hot in June before."

"Another good reason to open some windows in here," snapped Morgan as she slid one down with a loud bang.

"Maybe we should all go jump in the Harbor," said Emily as she headed to the back of the bus where she'd been cutting fabric for Morgan. "To cool ourselves off that is." She sat down on the bed and picked up the scissors and started cutting out what would become another curtain. Morgan was teaching her how to sew and had even promised to show her how to use the sewing machine this week — after she mastered cutting, which wasn't as easy as Emily had expected.

"That's a great idea," Morgan called from the front of the bus where her sewing machine was set up on the small table. "We should go down to the beach today — get in this good weather while it's here."

"Yeah," agreed Amy. "Don't forget this is Oregon … it could be raining by next week."

"We could take a picnic lunch down with us," suggested Morgan.

"Yeah, but let's get the rest of the junk cleared out of here first," said Carlie. "That will make finishing up the cleaning a whole lot easier."

"I thought we already cleared it all out," said Amy.

Emily glanced down the bus to see that Amy still hadn't budged from her comfy position on the couch. In fact that seemed to be her favorite spot. Emily shook her head and returned to measuring another eighteen-inch square — this one to be used for a pillow top. She didn't want to say anything, but she was starting to suspect that Amy Ngo was a little bit spoiled, not to mention slightly lazy. But Emily still felt like the new kid around here. Better to watch her mouth than to step on any toes.

"Yeah," said Carlie. "I thought so too, but then I looked under that bed and —"

"*Under* the bed?" Emily leaned over from her perch on the bed and peered under the bed at what appeared to be a solid wooden platform. "How can there be anything under here?" She knocked on the wood as if to prove her point.

"My dad showed it to me last night," explained Carlie, "while he was helping us to connect the electricity." The girls had gotten permission from Mr. Greeley to run a long outdoor extension cord from Carlie's house, which was only about thirty feet away. They couldn't use too much juice at a time, but it would provide enough to keep the little refrigerator running along with a light or Morgan's sewing machine.

"Here, I'll show you," Carlie said as she came to the back of the bus. "Hop off for a minute."

Emily slid off the bed and waited as Carlie bent over and hefted up the foot end of the bed. Once lifted, a spring mechanism attached beneath the plywood board caused the bed to fold into the wall. "See," said Carlie.

"Wow!" said Emily, peering down into what looked like a giant storage box. It was full of old-looking stuff. "Who knew?"

"Apparently my dad did. He said his parents used to have a motor home with the same kind of thing."

"It's so great that your dad's been helping us," said Emily, trying not to feel jealous of the fact that Carlie had such a cool dad. Emily's own father was an alcoholic who hit her mom — a lot. Emily, her brother, and their mom finally ran away with only the clothes on their backs to escape him. With a new last name, they hoped he wouldn't find them and take them back. So far so good.

"Yeah," said Carlie. He's going to take a look at the water system this weekend. He thinks we might even be able to use the sink and toilet."

"I want to see," said Amy, pushing past Emily to look under the bed.

"Me too," said Morgan.

Now all four girls crowded into the small bedroom area looking down into the random mix of boxes and things that were packed beneath it. So far the only things they'd removed from the bus had been rotten old curtains and nasty old bedding — things that had smelled musty or been chewed on by rodents. And right now that junk was bagged into garbage sacks, piled outside of the bus, and ready for the dumpster. But so far they hadn't seen anything like this. This stuff looked interesting.

"That looks like somebody's *personal* things," said Morgan.

Emily bent down and pulled out an old wooden apple crate filled with dusty vinyl record albums. "Jefferson Airplane?" she read the strange name on the cover and then flipped to another. "Bread? Who are these people anyway?"

"Weird," said Amy. "Do you suppose all this junk belongs to Mr. Greeley?"

"Hey, this isn't junk," said Morgan with real interest. She picked an album out of the crate and studied the back of it. "My mom had some of these vinyl records too. She almost gave them away, but I begged them from her. I've actually started collecting LPs for myself, and I happen to think they are totally cool."

"Want 'em?" asked Emily, holding the crate out to Morgan.

"Not so fast," said Amy. "What do you mean by 'collecting' them, Morgan? Are they valuable or something?"

Morgan shrugged. "Only to people who like them and collect them."

"Well, my sister An watches *The Antiques Road Show* all the time," said Amy. "And she keeps telling us that all kinds of junky looking things could be valuable."

"The most I've seen any of my albums going for, like on eBay, is only about ten to twenty bucks."

"Even so, maybe they should stay with the bus," said Amy. "I mean, since the bus belongs to all of us."

"I don't have a problem with that," said Morgan, slipping the album back into the crate. "But I don't know how we'll listen to them in here."

"What about this thing?" said Carlie, bending over to pick up what looked like some old-fashioned kind of music box. She held up the box and blew dust from the black plastic top causing Amy to sneeze.

"Bless you!" said Emily, stifling a giggle.

"It's a turntable!" exclaimed Morgan as she looked inside. "I wonder if it still works."

"I wonder what else is in here?" Emily stooped to pull out a cardboard box of books, both paperback and some older looking ones in hardback. She thumbed through the titles, noticing that there was a mix of mysteries, classics, and even some poetry collections — all which she happened to love. "Hey, these look pretty good." She glanced over to the built-in bookshelf over the back window. "Should I put them up there?"

"Take them outside and clean the dust off first," commanded Amy.

"Want me to use *Lysol*?" Emily teased as she carried the box toward the door. She didn't want to leave their unexpected treasure hunt, but it was getting stuffy and crowded in there. "Maybe we should take it all outside," she called over her shoulder, "to clean it off and get a better look."

So it was decided that they would empty out all the strange contents from the secret storage space beneath the bed. They hauled it outside to carefully examine each item, deciding upon its fate in the fresh air and sunshine. A lot of the things, like musty old clothes and mildewed tennis shoes, went straight into the trash, but other things, like the records and books, really did appear to be worth salvaging.

"It looks like these things belonged to a guy," said Amy as she gingerly dropped a dirty-looking baseball glove into the rapidly growing trash pile.

"Hey, don't throw that away," said Morgan, grabbing up the mitt as well as several other sports items that she suspected Amy had just tossed there. "These things might be collectable too. At least they look old."

"I can't imagine old sports junk will be worth anything," said Amy with an upturned nose. "Besides, we can't keep *all* this smelly stuff in the bus. We won't have enough room."

"Yeah, we will," said Morgan. "Under the bed, remember?"

"Yes, but why waste the space?" argued Amy. "We can use that to store other things."

"What other things?" asked Morgan.

"Hey, look at this," said Emily as she pulled what appeared to be a high school yearbook from the book box. "Boscoe Bay Cougars, 1979."

"Wow, that's a long time ago," said Morgan, peering over Emily's shoulder to see the cover of the faded red book. "Do you think it belonged to Mr. Greeley?"

"No way," said Amy, snatching the book from Emily. "Whoever owned this yearbook couldn't be much older than forty-five by now. And Mr. Greeley looks like he's about seventy. Maybe even older."

"The mental math whiz-kid strikes again," says Morgan, grabbing the yearbook from Amy and handing it back to Emily. "But I think she's right."

"Let's look at it," said Emily. She sat down on the sandy ground and flipped the cover open to expose a plain white page with several notes on it in various kinds of handwriting.

"Looks like this annual's been signed," said Amy.

"Maybe we can discover a clue as to whose this was." Emily sat down on the sandy soil and began to study the pages. The others joined her and soon they were reading the inscriptions out loud.

"'To Dan the man,'" read Morgan, "'Will miss you on the football field. Tight ends rule! Rick Byers.'"

"What's that supposed mean?" said Amy. "Tight ends rule?"

"It's a football position," explained Morgan.

"'Oh, Danny Boy ...'" read Emily. "'I wish I'd gotten to know you better ... Hang in there. Love, April.'" Emily laughed. "April with three hearts beneath her name!"

"She had it bad for Dan the man," laughed Amy.

"'Dan, Glad you seniors are leaving so the rest of us can have a chance at stardom too. Ten-four, good buddy, Dave Cross.'" Morgan laughed.

"'You should smile more — ,'" read Carlie, "'it increases your face value. Love and kisses, Kathy.'" They all laughed.

"Sounds like Dan the man was one hot guy," said Emily.

"Speaking of hot," said Morgan. "I'm cooking out here!"

"Me too," said Amy. "I thought we were going to take a picnic to the beach and go swimming."

"That's right!" said Carlie. "Let's hurry and get this stuff cleaned up and back on the bus."

"I know," said Morgan. "You guys finish putting this stuff back in the bus, and I'll go see what Grandma and I can throw together for a picnic lunch — that is unless anyone else has a better plan."

"That sounds awesome," said Emily as she returned the yearbook to the box of books.

"Then we can run home and get our swimsuits and stuff and meet back here," said Amy.

"I'll swing by your house, Morgan," offered Emily. "To help carry the picnic stuff."

They quickly put things back in the bus and took off to their own houses to change. But Emily couldn't quit thinking about this Dan guy as she pulled on the blue swimsuit that Morgan had given her when she found out Emily had only one outfit. Who was he anyway? And why was his yearbook in Mr. Greeley's bus? Not that these questions really bugged her. No, not at all. Because Emily loved a mystery. And it looked like the girls had not only inherited a bus but a mystery as well!

chapter two

The Harbor water was shockingly cold at first, but the girls splashed in and out of the waves until they were thoroughly cooled off. Then they spread out their towels and blankets over the warm sand and opened the cooler that Emily and Morgan had carried down to the Rainbow Bus. At the bus, Carlie had insisted that she and Amy do their part by transporting it the rest of the way to the beach.

Emily didn't even feel guilty when Amy complained about how heavy the cooler was. She thought it was about time that the girl did her share. During their massive cleanup of the trailer park, Emily had just assumed that Amy was working as hard as the rest of them, but the more she thought about it, the more she remembered seeing Amy sitting in the shade or sipping on a soda or complaining about a broken fingernail.

"This is the life," said Morgan, lying back on her towel, a can of Sierra Mist balancing on her chest. The can matched perfectly with Morgan's lime green, one-piece suit.

"Yeah, I'm ready for some downtime," said Carlie as she straightened out her beach towel. "I mean, isn't this supposed to be summer *vacation*? And we've been working harder than ever the last couple of weeks."

"But our work has a good payoff," said Morgan. "Don'cha think?"

"I do," said Emily, stretching her pale arms out into the sun's warmth. Hopefully she'd start getting a tan before too long. She glanced at her three friends lounging around her on their towels and blankets. It wasn't going to be easy hanging with these girls all summer. Morgan's naturally brown skin glowed like copper in the sunlight. Carlie's deep olive complexion, as well as the way she was filling out her tankini, looked amazing, and even Amy with her relatively fair Asian skin looked a lot tanner than Emily.

Emily flopped back onto her towel and hoped that it hadn't been a mistake to come here without sunscreen.

"Better watch out, Emily," warned Amy as she reached in her beach bag. Then almost as if Amy had been reading her thoughts, she pulled out a tube of sunscreen and tossed it to her. "You need to protect your skin from the sun. My sister An made me put some on before I came down here. And it's waterproof too."

"Thanks," said Emily.

"Yeah, you could be a lobster in no time," said Amy as she adjusted the strap of her bathing suit top. Amy was the only one to wear a two-piece, but her figure was so much like that of an eight-year-old, it didn't seem too risqué.

"But I do want to get some tan," said Emily as she cautiously smeared some of the white glop onto her ghostly white legs.

"You could *use* a little bit of tan, girlfriend," teased Morgan. "You are one pale white chick."

"Thanks a lot." Emily tried to spread the gooey sunscreen even thinner now.

"I'll take some of that too," said Morgan when she was done. "If Amy doesn't mind."

"*You* use sunscreen?" Amy tipped back her oversized sunglasses and stared at Morgan.

Morgan nodded her head. "Yes, Amy dear." She spoke as if addressing a four-year-old. "People of color can burn in the sun too."

So, before long, all four girls had on sunscreen. And for some unexplainable reason this made Emily feel better. She lay back down, but instantly wished she'd brought along a book to read. Why hadn't she grabbed one of those paperback mysteries from the bus?

"Wanna make a sandcastle?" asked Morgan after the girls had lazed around for about half an hour or so.

"No way," said Amy. "Leave me alone — I'm almost asleep."

"Me too," said Carlie.

"I'm game," said Emily, relieved to get up since she was already bored, plus the sun was intense. "Although, as you already know, I'm not very creative."

"Maybe not when it comes to art," admitted Morgan as she went over to where some driftwood and things were strewn up against the sandbank. "But I've seen some of your poetry, remember? That was creative."

"Don't you want to build the castle closer to the water?" asked Emily.

"Sure. But we need some props and things to take down there."

"Oh." So Emily followed Morgan's lead by gathering up sticks and rocks and shell pieces until their hands were full, then they went down to the wet sand to select their building site.

Emily wasn't the least surprised when Morgan began drawing an outline and giving instructions for how to proceed. And, trusting Morgan's artistic sense, Emily just did as she was told.

After about an hour, their castle was nearly complete and Amy and Carlie came over to check it out.

"Wow," said Carlie. "That's awesome."

"Yeah," admitted Amy. "Not bad."

"Want to help?" asked Morgan.

"Sure," said Carlie. "How?"

And so Morgan gave them both assignments to gather more round little stones, some four-inch twigs, and any sort of seashell that they could find.

"Do you really need that stuff?" asked Emily. "Or were you just trying to get rid of them?"

Morgan laughed. "We haven't been friends that long, but you sure seem to know me pretty well."

Still, Morgan managed to put their items to good use when they returned about twenty minutes later.

"*Voila!*" she said, standing up and stretching her back. "Finished."

"It's a work of art," said Emily as she gave her a high five.

"Man, I wish I had a photo of it," said Morgan.

"I could run and get my camera," offered Carlie.

"Cool."

"You guys stay here and protect it," Carlie was already taking off. "I'll be back in ten minutes."

"And she will," said Morgan. "I've seen that girl run."

"You should enter the sandcastle-building contest next weekend," said Amy. "I remember reading about it in the newspaper last week."

"Oh, yeah," said Emily. "My mom was telling me about that. They're hosting the contest at the resort where she works. She said that people are coming from all over. It's the first one in Boscoe Bay, and they want it to become an annual event."

"Of course, there's a registration fee," said Amy.

"How much?" asked Morgan.

"I think it was twenty-five dollars."

Morgan frowned. "That seems stupid. Just to build a sandcastle when you can do it for free right here?"

"Yeah, but there are prizes," said Amy. "The first place winner gets five-hundred dollars."

"Five-hundred dollars?" Morgan looked seriously interested now.

"And there are second- and third-place prizes too," said Amy. "I can't remember how much."

"There's Carlie," said Morgan, pointing to where the trail came onto the beach. "Right on time."

Carlie shot the sandcastle from a variety of angles. Then, as a middle-aged couple came walking down the beach, Amy approached them to ask if they'd take a photo of the four girls with the sculpture. The couple gladly agreed, complimenting the beauty of the sandcastle as the girls posed behind it for several shots.

"You girls are very talented," the man said, handing the camera back.

"Yes," said Amy. "We think we should enter the sandcastle-building contest at Boscoe Bay Resort."

He nodded. "I'm sure you'd have a good chance."

As the couple walked away, Amy turned to Morgan. "Why don't we?"

"We?" Morgan pushed her glasses up the bridge of her nose and frowned at Amy.

Amy nodded. "Yes, we. We could all chip in on the entry fee, and you could tell us what to do." She smirked at

Morgan. "Which you seem to enjoy doing anyway. That would only be six dollars twenty-five cents apiece to enter the contest."

Morgan laughed. "You have it all figured out."

"And one hundred twenty-five dollars apiece if we win first place," said Amy.

Suddenly all four girls were very interested. They all started talking at once. Some thought they should put their winnings into fixing up the bus. Some thought they should just split it and call it good. Then they talked about a compromise — half for the bus and half to split equally.

"Let's go back to the Rainbow Bus and start planning our strategy," said Morgan as she turned around and headed back to their sunbathing spot on the beach.

"Yes," agreed Amy, right on her heels. "And we'll need to fill out the entry form."

"And I'll have to start sketching some designs."

"I can provide the tools," said Carlie. "We have lots of shovels and rakes and stuff."

Emily thought about what she could contribute to the efforts but, as usual, she was coming up short.

"Okay," said Morgan. "I will agree to this only if Emily can be my right-hand man. I mean, girl."

"Why's that?" asked Amy in a somewhat insulted-sounding tone.

"Because Emily totally gets me," said Morgan. "And she's good at following directions."

"Hey, I don't have a problem with that," said Carlie in her usual agreeable way.

"Okay," agreed Amy with some reluctance. "I guess I'm okay with it."

So maybe Emily did have something to offer the group. At least she hoped so as she picked up one handle of the cooler. "Why don't you help me with this, Amy?" she said, waiting for Amy to protest.

"Okay," said Amy. "But only because Morgan provided the lunch and Carlie has her camera junk to carry."

And the four of them trekked down the trail and over the dunes and back to the Rainbow Bus, which was surprisingly cool when they got inside.

"Not bad," said Amy, immediately taking the couch.

"Siesta time," said Carlie, heading back to the bed.

"Room for two more?" grinned Morgan.

"Sure," said Carlie. "This is one big bed."

The three of them found their spots and within no time everyone was fast asleep, with Carlie even snoring. Well, everyone except Emily. For some reason she was wide awake. She just lay there for a while, thinking about the strangeness of her life these past few weeks.

Just the fact that she was here right now with her three new friends — sharing this cool clubhouse of an old bus, hanging out on the beach together, building sandcastles, planning to enter contests — was mind blowing in itself.

But when she replayed the events of the past couple of weeks — dealing with bullies, fixing up the rundown trailer park, getting the hand-me-down clothes and colorful things for her room from Morgan — she couldn't believe her good fortune. And the most amazing thing … inviting Jesus into her heart at church! Everything was so different from her old life — less than a month ago — back when everything looked totally bleak and hopeless. She closed her eyes and whispered a thank-you prayer, then rolled over on her stomach, hoping her mind would shut down for a while and let her sleep.

Then she spied the box of books down on the floor beside her. She was about to pull out one of those mysteries, but instead her hand paused on the spine of the faded, red yearbook. She still wondered about this Dan guy. Who was he and why was his high school yearbook hidden here? Was it just a coincidence or did he have something to do with this bus?

She pulled out the book and opened it up to the page with all the writing from his friends, glancing over it again, hoping to find some hidden clue as to who this guy was — who he might be now. He certainly seemed to be well liked. And, it occurred to her that he might even be missing this yearbook.

"Watcha doing?" whispered Morgan.

"Just looking at this," whispered Emily. She rolled onto her back, holding up the yearbook.

"Oh, yeah. Dan the man." Morgan sat up and leaned against the wall behind them. "Find anything new?"

"Not really …" She scooted up and sat beside her, continuing to whisper although it looked like Carlie was sound asleep. "I mean, we know that he's well liked … by both guys and girls. And he's good at sports."

"Let's look through the yearbook and see if we can find his photo."

"But we don't know his last name yet," pointed out Emily.

"Well, how many Dans can there be?" asked Morgan. "And we know he's a senior."

"Go to the senior section," said Amy.

Both Morgan and Emily looked up, surprised.

"And make room for me," commanded Amy, squeezing in next to Emily.

"Hey," said Carlie, nearly falling off the bed. "What's going on?"

"An earthquake," said Morgan. "Hang on for dear life."

"Wake up, sleepyhead," said Amy. "Nap time's over."

Carlie sat up and yawned. "What's going on?"

"We're looking for Dan the man," said Morgan.

"Huh?" Carlie blinked then looked over at the yearbook. "Oh."

They huddled together as they turned page after page, joking as they noticed some pretty weird hair and clothing styles.

"I have two words for these guys," said Carlie, finally waking up as she pointed to a guy named Carl, whose long, fluffy blond hair made him look like a girl. *"Hair cut."*

"I think that's one word," said Emily.

"Yeah, whatever," said Carlie. "Get out the scissors."

"Here's a Daniel Foster," said Morgan, pointing to a skinny guy with curly hair and wire-rimmed glasses. "Do you think that's him?"

"He looks kind of nerdy to me," said Emily.

"Not exactly the jock type," added Carlie.

"But everyone looks kind of strange in this year-book," said Morgan. "It might be hard to tell what they're really like."

"Well, keep going," said Amy. "But stick your finger there."

So they flipped through the pages and were about to give up when Emily pointed to the bottom of the last page of pictures. *"Dan Watterson,"* she proclaimed. "I'll bet that's him. *Dan the man."*

"Even with his long hair, he's pretty good-looking," observed Amy.

"And he looks big too, like he could be athletic," said Morgan.

"There should be an index with more photos listed for him in the back of the yearbook," Amy said with authority.

"How do you know that?" asked Carlie.

"Because my brother and sisters have high school annuals, silly. I've looked at them before."

Sure enough, there was an index. And beneath Dan Watterson's name was a list of about a dozen more page numbers. They retraced their steps back through the yearbook finding shot after shot of Dan Watterson: football hero … basketball star … He even played baseball. And when he wasn't in a sports photo, he had a girl or two hanging on his arm.

"But I still don't get this," said Emily. "Why is this guy's yearbook in our bus?"

"Maybe it was his bus," suggested Amy.

"Dan the man?" said Emily. "Living in a funky old bus like this?" She shook her head. "It just doesn't add up."

"And why would Mr. Greeley have this bus?" said Carlie. "I mean, if it belonged to Dan Watterson?"

"It does seem a little weird," admitted Morgan.

"Maybe Dan is Mr. Greeley's son," suggested Emily.

"But his name is wrong," Amy pointed out.

Emily considered this. Sometimes names were wrong. For instance her own last name wasn't really Adams … but this was top secret. Other than Morgan, no one in Boscoe Bay knew her family's story.

"And here's what's been bugging me," said Carlie. "Why did Mr. Greeley have this bus here — I mean, for all this time?"

"We don't know how long it's been here," Morgan pointed out.

"Well, you saw the big heap of dead blackberry vines that Mr. Greeley removed," said Carlie.

"That's probably what he was doing while we were cleaning up the trailer court," said Amy. "Remember how he was gone all the time?"

"Anyway," continued Carlie, "that suggests that the bus has been around here a few years."

"That and all the dust," added Emily.

"Plus all the stuff that we found under the bed," said Carlie. "It reminds me of those boxes that people put stuff in and bury, you know ... what are they called?"

"You mean a time capsule?" said Morgan.

"Yeah. Like a time capsule from ..." Carlie tapped her finger on the cover of the yearbook, "a time capsule from 1979!"

Emily nodded. "She's right. It does."

"Do you think the bus has been here that long?" asked Morgan.

No one answered.

"I wonder why ..." said Emily. "Why was it parked back here in the first place?"

"Maybe it was a friend of Mr. Greeley's," said Morgan.

"Then why did he leave it here?" persisted Emily.

"Maybe we'll never know," said Amy, hopping off of the bed. "But don't forget, we have things to do if we're going to enter the sandcastle-building contest. Remember, it's only a few days away."

"Let's put these boxes and things away first," said Morgan. "It's getting pretty crowded in here."

"I'll take care of it," offered Emily. "You go ahead and get your sketch pad out and —"

"See," said Morgan, patting Emily on the back. "That's why she's my right-hand girl."

"And I'll go see if can find that old newspaper," said Amy.

Carlie looked at her watch. "I have to go home now. I'm supposed to watch my brothers while Mom goes grocery shopping."

"Let's reconvene back here after dinner tonight," suggested Amy.

Morgan handed Emily the key, which was now hanging on a hand-beaded necklace created by Morgan. "You lock up, Em."

The girls agreed, and just like that the bus was evacuated — except for Emily who continued to carefully replace the boxes and things back beneath the bed. At least there was plenty of room now. And for the most part, the dust and grime had been cleaned. She was tempted to hang around and put the books up on the shelf. But she felt a little guilty for being in the bus by herself. The girls hadn't really made any rules yet, but this was supposed to be a clubhouse to be shared, not Emily's own private retreat. Even if she wished it could be.

She put the book box in last, standing before the still-opened bed as she tried to imagine what kind of a person this Dan Watterson really was and whether or not this bus had actually belonged to him. She'd noticed his name inside some of the other books and suspected that everything they'd discovered today had at one time belonged to Dan.

As she locked up the bus and slowly walked back to her house, she wondered something else too. If all that old keepsake kind of stuff really did belong to Dan Watterson — whoever he was — why didn't he want it back? And why had it all ended up in Mr. Greeley's possession? If she wasn't so intimidated by Mr. Greeley's grumpy personality, she might be tempted to ask. As it was, this might be a mystery she'd have to solve on her own.

By the time they regrouped after dinner, Morgan had drawn several sketches for possible sandcastles. And everyone seemed to have a different opinion.

"I like the French one," said Carlie. "It reminds me of a fairy tale. I expect to see a dragon coming around the corner."

"But it's so expected," said Amy. "I'll bet half the sandcastles on the beach will look just like it. We need something special, something that will stand out."

"Why not the English castle," said Morgan. "I thought we could do all kinds of things with that open courtyard." She glanced at Carlie. "You could be in charge of landscaping."

"But it's so boxy looking," said Carlie.

Determined to not get into the middle of this, Emily was carefully reading the article about the contest from the newspaper that Amy had brought. "Hey," she said suddenly. "It says here that you can make *anything* — well, as long as it's not obscene. It's supposed to be 'family appropriate.'"

"Like I would design an *obscene* sandcastle!" Morgan rolled her eyes.

"But the thing is, it doesn't have to be a sand*castle*. Listen." And Emily proceeded to read how a winner from a similar contest had sculpted a ten-foot-long mermaid.

"A mermaid," said Carlie. "That'd be pretty."

"Someone's already done that, silly," said Amy.

"Good work, Em," said Morgan, pointing to the paper. "That's why she's my right-hand girl."

"Enough with the right-hand girl stuff already," said Amy.

"Yeah," said Carlie. "Like what are we? Chopped liver?"

They all laughed.

"Okay, let's get serious," said Morgan. "Everyone think really hard … what would be cool as a sand sculpture?"

"How about a seahorse?" said Amy.

"Good, but too easy," said Morgan.

"A dragon?" suggested Carlie.

"Maybe …" Morgan considered this.

"Maybe I should make a list," said Amy, snatching up her notebook. "Then we can vote."

"How about an angel?" said Carlie.

"Or a tyrannosaurus rex?" suggested Emily.

"How about a submarine?" said Morgan. "One that's just coming out of the water, but it's really on the beach."

"What about a pirate ship?" said Amy.

"How about SpongeBob SquarePants?" said Emily, and they all laughed.

"Slow down," said Amy. "I'm still on submarine."

"Hey, that's not a bad idea," said Morgan.

"The submarine?" said Carlie. "That was your idea, Morgan."

"No. SpongeBob SquarePants."

"I was just kidding," admitted Emily.

"But, seriously, it would be funny. And who else would do something like that?"

"And," Emily held up the newspaper, pointing to a line. "I just noticed here that you only have three hours to build it."

"Three hours?" echoed Morgan. "That would rule out pirate ships, dinosaurs, and submarines. They're way too complicated for three hours."

"But SpongeBob SquarePants isn't complicated."

"Go ahead and sketch it out for us," urged Amy. "Let's see what it would look like."

Morgan started sketching a square on two legs then laughed. "I'll have to watch cartoons to remember exactly how he looks. It's no good unless you get it right."

"But he's got those skinny little legs." Emily pointed to the sticks protruding from the pants. "How can he possibly stand up if he's made of sand?"

"Maybe he can be sitting down," suggested Carlie. "Like on a piece of driftwood?"

"Or maybe he's sunbathing with his little friends," said Morgan with excitement. "Remember, he has a crab and a snail and —"

"A starfish!" exclaimed Emily.

"That'll be perfect for the beach."

"Yeah," said Morgan "and they can have a picnic basket and suntan lotion and everything."

"It'll be so cool."

"And sure to win," said Amy. As Amy mentally divided up their winnings, Emily imagined seeing dollar signs in her eyes. "Let's fill out the application." She snatched the paper from Emily and started to fill in the blanks. "Uh-oh," she said suddenly.

"What?" they all asked.

"There's a deadline, you guys."

"When?"

"Tomorrow." She smiled. "Not a moment too soon, huh? Almost like destiny." She turned and looked at them. "Did you guys bring your money for the fee?"

To Emily's relief, they hadn't. But she suspected they'd have it together before she would. Maybe even by tonight. And while she knew that $6.25 wouldn't seem like anything more than chump change to most people, it was $6.25 more than she had at the moment. She knew she could ask her mom, but she also knew how tight things were right now. She'd been afraid to ask her mom for anything lately.

"Hey, maybe your mom could turn the application in for us, Emily," said Morgan. "Since she works there. That way we'd make the deadline for sure."

"Yeah, how about if we drop our money off by your house before your mom goes to work tomorrow?" suggested Amy.

"Sure," said Emily, trying to think of a quick way to earn six dollars and twenty-five cents by morning. At least she wouldn't have to be humiliated by admitting to her friends that she was broke. At least not right now anyway. It was such a pain being poor!

It was getting late now and time to call it a day. "My mom and brother usually leave the house a little before nine to get to work on time," she told them. They all promised to drop off their part of the deposit before then.

"Here's the key," said Emily, handing the precious key back to Morgan as they stepped outside.

"I don't see why Morgan gets to have total control of the key," said Amy. "I mean, doesn't the bus belong to all of us equally?"

"Yeah, of course," said Morgan. "I'm just keeping it because Mr. Greeley gave it to me."

"But that's just it," continued Amy. "Why do you get to keep it all the time?"

"Why not?" asked Carlie.

"Because it's not fair," said Amy.

"Why not?" demanded Emily. "Morgan was the one who led us in the cleanup of Harbor View. She's the one who wasn't afraid to talk to Mr. Greeley. Why shouldn't she be in charge of the key?"

"Yeah," said Carlie.

"Because we should vote," said Amy.

"Vote?" echoed Morgan. "On what?"

"On who's really in charge here."

"In charge?" Morgan frowned at Amy. "Like someone should be the dictator? I thought we were all friends ... and equals."

"Yes," said Amy quickly. "We are. But we're also a club. And a club has a president."

"You think we have to have a president?" said Carlie.

Amy nodded. "Yes. And I think we should have an election."

Emily sighed and Morgan groaned and Carlie just laughed.

"Come on you guys," Amy urged them. "If we're going to be a real club, we should take ourselves seriously. We need someone who's smart and able to make decisions to lead us. And I think I'd be perfect for the job."

They all laughed, except for Amy. Her eyes began to tear and her chin quivered.

"I'm sorry, Amy," said Morgan. "But I just don't see the —"

"I knew you wouldn't," she snapped. "You guys really don't like me, do you? I know it's probably because I'm the youngest one here. But I can't help it if I skipped a grade. I can't help it that I'm smarter than average. But does that mean I should be persecuted?"

"No," said Morgan. "Of course not."

"I don't mind if we have an election," said Carlie.

"Me neither," said Emily.

"In fact, we can do it right now if you want," said Morgan.

"No way," said Amy. "We need to nominate first. Then we campaign and make speeches and finally we vote — by secret ballot."

Morgan groaned again. "That's so much work."

"But it's the right way to do it," protested Amy. "And I'll bring paper and stuff. You guys just be ready to cooperate. Okay?"

With reluctance they all agreed. And as they walked back to their houses, Emily imagined that Amy was probably a natural leader after all. Except that she was sort of a dictator. Emily wasn't so sure they were ready for that. But why should she worry? Morgan would easily be elected three to one.

The girls told each other good night, and Emily unlocked her front door and went inside. As usual, Mom and Kyle wouldn't be home for a couple more hours. Emily was used to it now. And at least the place didn't look nearly as dismal and empty as it had when they first moved in. She looked around the house and realized that it had gotten pretty messy this past week. With Mom and Kyle working so many hours and Emily's recent projects with her friends, things had been neglected here.

Maybe that's how she could earn some quick cash. She kicked her idea into high gear as she went about cleaning up and straightening in the living room. She picked up soda cans, newspapers, and dirty socks. She dusted the few pieces of furniture that Morgan's mom had donated. She plumped the pillows. And finally — since they didn't have a vacuum cleaner yet — she actually got down on her hands and knees to pick up lint and crumbs from the dingy tan carpeting. After that she attacked the kitchen.

By the time Mom and Kyle got home, the place looked great. Well, as great as a somewhat rundown double-wide mobile home could look.

"Hey," said Mom as she came in the door and kicked off her shoes. "Someone cleaned up in here."

Emily smiled at her.

"What's the big occasion?" asked Kyle. "Are we having a party?"

Emily shrugged. "No. I just thought this place could use some help."

Her mom hugged her. "Thanks, sweetie. I appreciate it."

Emily wanted to hit her mom up for some cash now, but after hearing her gratitude, she wasn't so sure she wanted to spoil everything. She hated looking like she'd only done it for money ... even if it was the truth.

"I'm so tired," said Mom. "Such a long day. Do you guys mind if I just take a shower and call it a night?"

"Not at all," said Emily. This had been the norm since they'd moved here. "I've been busy today too and I'm tired."

"When are we going to get a TV?" asked Kyle as he poured a glass of milk.

"Hey, I almost forgot. Rita from the restaurant offered me an old TV that her mother-in-law gave her. She said it's in a cabinet that's as big as a house. I told her we have lots of room and that we'll pick it up this weekend."

"This weekend?" complained Kyle. "I'd be happy to go over and pick it up tonight."

"It's too late," said Mom.

"How about tomorrow?" he begged. "Please, Mom. I've been working hard and I'm so bored that I'm about to go nuts. You don't want me to start running around to find some excitement at night, do you?"

She shook her head. "No, of course not. And you have been working hard." She was starting to cry. "You've both been working hard. I'm so proud of you —"

"Yeah, yeah," said Kyle. "I wasn't looking for thanks. Just say I can pick up that TV. I mean, like ASAP."

"I'll talk with Rita tomorrow," she promised.

Before Emily went to bed, she read from the little New Testament that Morgan had given her. Then she prayed, finally asking God to help her to get six dollars and twenty-five cents by morning.

By 8:30 the next morning, all three girls had stopped by Emily's house to drop off their share of the entry fee. She thanked them and assured them that her mom would drop it off for them.

"What's all that about?" asked Mom as she rinsed out her coffee cup and set it in the sink.

"The sandcastle contest," said Emily, holding out the slightly rumpled application from the newspaper.

"Huh?" Mom glanced at it then looked surprised. "You mean the one at the resort? *This* weekend?"

Emily nodded. "Me and my friends want to enter."

"My friends and I," her mom corrected.

"You too?" teased Emily.

Mom smiled warmly and took the paper. "But there's a fee, Emily. Twenty-five dollars."

"I know." Emily scooped out the bills and change that she'd been collecting in her pocket and set it on the counter. "We have most of it already."

"Most?"

"All except for my share."

"How much is that?"

"Six dollars and twenty-five cents."

Mom nodded. "Well, how about if I cover you on that?"

"Really?"

"Sure. We're not totally penniless, Emily. And you've been doing such a great job of helping out. I'm so proud of the work you and your friends did for the trailer court. Hey, I'm happy to contribute."

"And we might win," said Emily hopefully. "Morgan is our designer, and she's really creative."

Mom smiled. "Yes, she definitely is. But I've heard that some very experienced sand sculptors are coming to town. And some people are really serious about this competition, honey. They practice all year long and go all over the country."

"But we'll still have a chance," said Emily with confidence. "Can you turn this in for us? Today is the deadline."

"No problem. I just happen to be going that way."

Emily put her arms around her mom. "Thanks, Mom."

Mom laughed. "No problem."

"I mean, for everything," said Emily. "For getting us here to Boscoe Bay and for working so hard. I think it's all totally worth it."

Mom nodded. "I do too. It's just been a little hard starting out with nothing."

"Ready to go?" called Kyle from the backdoor.

And then they were gone, just like every other day, and Emily had the house to herself. She straightened up the kitchen and wrote in her journal for a little while, but it was barely ten o'clock and she was already feeling bored. She wondered when Amy planned on holding their little election today. And since they still didn't have a phone connected, Emily decided the only way to find out was to go to Morgan's house. Of course, any excuse to go to Morgan's was a good excuse. She felt more at home at the Evans' than at her own home — mostly because there was always someone there. Plus, there was usually something good to eat.

"Come in, Em," called Morgan when Emily knocked on the screen door. Morgan was sitting on the living-room floor with a large tray of beads between her legs. "How's it going?" she asked, pushing her glasses up the bridge of her nose as she looked at Emily.

"Okay." Emily sat down beside her. "Whatcha doing?"

"Well, it was going to be a surprise ..."

"Oh. Want me to leave?"

"No. Why don't you stay and help me?"

Then Morgan showed her what she was doing. She had some alphabet beads along with some colored ones. "First you put on two purple beads, then two blue, two green, then yellow, orange, red, and finally magenta. See." She held up the leather string that was nearly half full of colorful beads.

"It looks like a rainbow," said Emily.

"Yeah." Now Morgan picked up a bead with the letter Y and slipped it on. This was followed by the letter A and N and another Y and finally L, which was really the beginning since Morgan had put the beads on backwards. Although it still didn't make sense. LYNAY."

"Who's Lynay?"

"It's a secret," said Morgan as she handed Emily a piece of string. "At least for now. So, can you make another one just like it?"

"Sure. Easy." And Emily followed the same pattern. Both girls worked quietly. Morgan showed Emily how to finish the pattern with another rainbow on the other side of the letters.

"That's pretty," said Emily. "But I'm curious about LYNAY."

The girls worked until they had four short strings of beads. "Finished," announced Morgan.

"What are they?"

Morgan wrapped one around Emily's wrist. "Bracelets."

"Cool."

"But it's a secret, okay?"

Emily nodded.

"Oh, yeah. Amy called and the big election is supposed to be at one o'clock today. Carlie had to babysit her brothers this morning. After the election, we're going down to the beach to practice our sand sculpture."

"Practice?"

"Yeah, we need to work on the size and who does what. Three hours isn't that long if we want it to look totally perfect. Want to see my drawing?"

"Sure."

Morgan pocketed the bracelets, picked up her beading tray, and led Emily to her bedroom where she produced a sketch pad with a detailed drawing of SpongeBob lying on a beach blanket with all of his little friends nearby.

"That is so cool," said Emily. "And it doesn't even look that complicated."

"But remember the sculpture is in 3-D."

"Three-D?"

"You know, everything is carved and it has to have depth and dimension. It's not like we can just draw it on the beach and be done. I'm guessing that SpongeBob will be about two feet high."

Emily nodded. "Yeah, I can see how we might need to practice it."

"Want to take these over to the bus?" asked Morgan as she held up some pillows that she'd sewn. Emily recognized the fabric squares that she had cut out. "I finished some curtains too. We can make a lunch and take them all over to the bus."

"Sure."

They made a quick lunch to take with them. Then, loaded up with pillows and curtains, they walked over to the bus. As Morgan unlocked the door, Emily asked if she thought it was okay to be at the bus when all four girls weren't there.

"I don't see why not," said Morgan. "But I guess I don't know how the others will feel about it. I suppose it does make sense to have this stupid election so that we can sort of know what to expect."

"Well, we know that you'll be the one elected," said Emily. "I'm sure voting for you."

"That doesn't mean it's a shoo-in," said Morgan. "I mean, Carlie has a vote too. And Amy might make some really good points as to why she should be president. What if I voted for her?"

"You wouldn't!"

Morgan laughed. "Probably not. But I'd have to be fair. If I was convinced that she would be best and if you guys were too ... well, I'd have to vote for her."

Emily shuddered to think what their club would be like if Amy were president. She imagined a horrible dictatorship where they'd all work hard, and Amy would sit around and tell them what to do. It wasn't that she didn't like Amy, but maybe she didn't totally trust her.

"It looks pretty good in here," said Emily after they'd hung the new curtains and put the new pillows on the couch.

"Yeah," said Morgan. "But I'd still like to make something for the bed. That blanket on the mattress just isn't cutting it for me. And I think it needs a whole bunch more pillows."

Emily laughed. "Well, I'm sure by the time you're done it will be so cool that Better Buses and Gardens will want to feature it in their magazine."

"Hello in there," called Carlie as she and Amy came into the bus.

"How long have you guys been here?" asked Amy.

"Just long enough to hang some curtains," said Morgan.

"Looks nice." Carlie looked around and nodded.

"Campaigning are we?" asked Amy.

"Are we?" replied Morgan, pointing to the button pinned on Amy's shirt. "Go with Ngo?"

Amy laughed. "Just wanted to show you guys that I believe in myself." She set an empty tissue box, a small pad of paper, and some pencils on the table.

"Should we get this over with?" asked Morgan as she picked up a pencil.

"Not so fast," said Amy, snatching the pencil back. "We need to do nominations first."

"I nominate Morgan," said Emily.

"Wait," said Amy. "We need to take notes."

"Notes?" said Morgan. "What is this? School?"

"If we're a club, we should take notes," said Amy. "Actually, I mean minutes. We should take minutes. Do I hear any volunteers?"

Emily held out her hand to take the notebook from Amy. "Here, I'll do it. Let's just get this show on the road. We need to get out to the beach and work on SpongeBob. You should see Morgan's drawing. It's really —"

"Not right now," said Amy. "First things first." She pointed to the couch. "Everyone sit down." Then she pointed to the table. "Emily, you sit there so you can take notes."

"Yes, sir," said Emily.

"Don't you mean minutes?" said Carlie with a snicker.

"You guys!" said Amy, losing her patience.

"Okay, okay." Morgan held up her hands as if to surrender and then sat down on the couch. "Go ahead, Amy."

"All right." Amy continued to stand. "Let's begin nominations."

"I nominate Morgan," said Carlie.

"For what?" said Amy with a scowl.

"For president, of course," said Carlie impatiently. "I thought that's what the election was for."

"But we should have other offices too," said Amy.

"Other offices?" Morgan frowned at her. "What is this now? The military?"

Amy nodded over to Emily. "We need a secretary to keep minutes. And we should have a treasurer," she added.

"What for?" asked Emily.

"What if we win the sandcastle contest?" said Amy. "We'll need to keep track of that money and how it's spent. And we might want to start having club dues."

"Dues?" Morgan frowned. "Why do we have to complicate everything?"

"Fine," snapped Amy. "Let's just elect you as president and you can call all the shots, Morgan."

"No …" Morgan shook her head. "Let's be fair."

"And let's get this over with," said Carlie.

"Okay," said Morgan. "I nominate Amy for president."

Amy smiled. "Thanks, Morgan."

"Okay," said Emily in an official-sounding voice. "We have two nominations for president. Do I hear a third?" No one said anything. "So, shall we consider nominations closed?"

"Yes," said Carlie.

"Hey, you're good at this, Emily," said Amy.

Emily smiled. "That's only because I was in student council back at my old school."

"Well, I nominate Emily for secretary," said Amy.

"Thank you," said Emily, writing down her own name. "Any other nominations?"

"I nominate Carlie," said Morgan.

"But what if I don't want to?" asked Carlie.

"Why not?" demanded Amy.

Carlie shrugged. "I don't like to write."

"You can decline the nomination," said Emily.

"Then I decline." Carlie grinned.

"Okay, then I nominate Carlie for treasurer," said Emily, feeling bad that Carlie hadn't been nominated yet.

Carlie frowned.

"You want to decline that too?" asked Emily.

She shrugged. "I guess not. But Amy is lots better in math than I am."

"But Amy is running for president," said Emily.

Morgan groaned. "And SpongeBob is waiting."

"Okay, okay." Emily looked down at the notebook. "Are nominations closed then?"

Everyone agreed that was enough, and so it was time for speeches. "You go first," Morgan said to Amy. "Since it looks like you're ready."

"Thank you," said Amy, standing up. "As you all know, I'm a little bit younger than you three. I won't be twelve until August. But you can't let my age or my size fool you. I skipped a grade because my IQ was extremely high and I was very far ahead of my class. As you know, I'm still ahead of our class. I've been the mental-math champion at our school for the past three years, and I've placed in district every year. I've won the last four spelling bees in our school as well as the last two years in district." Carlie yawned, and Amy frowned at her but continued. "I'm a gifted musician, playing flute, violin, and piano. I'm very self-disciplined, and I know a lot about business since my family owns a prominent restaurant downtown. I've lived in Harbor View Mobile-Home Court longer than any of you. I think you'll have to agree that I have all the qualifications to be president. I am a natural leader."

Emily looked down at her notebook and literally bit her tongue. Not hard though. Just enough to keep her from saying anything.

"Is that all?" asked Morgan.

"No," said Amy. "If I am elected president, I will take you all to dinner to celebrate — on me. Also, I will make sure that our club is run efficiently and in a way that will be appreciated by all." She made a little bow. "Thank you very much!"

Morgan started clapping and the other two followed.

"Next?" said Emily, looking at Morgan.

Morgan nodded without standing up. "Well, I think you guys know me. You know what I'm like and whether or not I'd make a good president. I encourage you to vote for whoever you think is right for the job. If you chose me, I'll do the best I can. But, as you know, I'm not perfect. Thanks."

"Is that all?" asked Emily. "You want to make a speech, Carlie?"

She shook her head.

"And I don't." Emily glanced at Amy. "Can we vote now?"

"Yes," said Amy as she handed out pencils and pieces of paper. "Cast your votes for president, secretary, and treasurer and then put them in the box."

"The Kleenex box?" teased Carlie.

Amy just made a face and began to write. Soon all ballots were cast into the Kleenex box.

"Why don't you read them, Emily," said Amy. "Since you are probably going to be secretary."

Emily opened up the papers and read them. No big surprises, but she hoped Amy's feelings wouldn't be hurt.

"Carlie has three votes for treasurer," she began. "And one is blank."

"I'll bet that was you." Morgan looked at Carlie.

"I have been chosen as secretary," said Emily. She looked at Morgan. "Unanimously."

Morgan clapped and the others did too.

"And for president," announced Emily, "three votes for Morgan and one for Amy, making Morgan Evans the first ever president of the Rainbow Bus. Congratulations, Morgan."

Amy frowned, but reached over and shook Morgan's hand. "I figured you'd win. Are you going to make a victory speech?"

"No," said Morgan. "But thanks, you guys." Then she reached in her pocket. "I have a little gift for everyone."

"Bribes?" said Amy with raised brows.

"Yeah, right," said Morgan. "After the votes were cast."

"Payoffs?" said Amy.

"Give it a rest, Amy," said Emily as she closed the notebook.

Morgan laughed. "They're not bribes or payoffs. They're just friendship bracelets. Emily helped me make them."

"Yeah," said Emily. "But I still don't know what they mean."

Morgan handed them out and the girls thanked her and tied them onto their wrists.

"They're pretty," said Carlie, "But what do the letters mean?"

"Who's Lynay?" asked Amy.

"It's an abbreviation for what I think should be the theme of our club," said Morgan. "And since I'm president, I'm going to recommend it. Of course, you guys can always refuse ..."

"What is it?" said Emily.

"LYNAY," said Morgan, "Stands for 'Love your neighbor as yourself.'"

"Oh," said Emily. "That's cool."

"I like it," said Carlie.

"Yeah," said Amy. "It's nice."

"The thing is ..." said Morgan seriously. "We need to love each other just like Jesus said to do. But we need to love each other just as well as we love ourselves — meaning we need to love ourselves too. Does that make sense?"

The girls agreed that it did.

"As your new president, I want to propose that to be the rule for our club," said Morgan.

"Just one rule?" Amy challenged. "You really think that's enough."

"I do," said Morgan.

"I don't know …" Amy looked unconvinced.

"Well, let's see how it works for a while anyway," said Morgan. "And I was thinking that we should keep it kind of a secret rule. Like a secret code, you know. I mean, we want to live it in our lives, but we don't have to tell anyone what the letters mean. It could be just between us."

"Cool," said Emily.

"Okay," said Amy.

"Great," said Carlie, standing up. "And now let's hit the beach. I've got tools and buckets and stuff outside."

"SpongeBob SquarePants, here we come," yelled Morgan as the girls poured out of the bus and headed over the dunes.

chapter five

You guys ready for this?" asked Morgan on Saturday morning as the four girls loaded their tools and stuff into the back of Emily's mom's van.

"We had it down pretty well yesterday," Carlie reminded her.

"Yeah," said Emily. "If we do it like we worked it out, we should be fine. But we all need to remember not to hurry — that's when we make mistakes. And everyone has to do their job."

"And no complaining," said Morgan.

Emily knew this comment was directed to Amy. Yesterday, she continued to find fault with their sculpture, but it was mostly because things weren't finished yet. When it was all done, even Amy had liked it.

"If we can just do it as well as yesterday," said Carlie, "I'll bet we'll have a good chance at winning."

"We'll do it even better," said Morgan. "Yesterday was just practice."

"We'll win for sure," said Amy.

Emily didn't mention what her mom had told her, about how there were some very experienced sculptors coming today.

"Imagine five-hundred," continued Amy in a dreamy voice. She nodded to Carlie now. "I hope that our new treasurer is ready to start calculating our winnings and the split and everything."

Carlie frowned and looked at Morgan. "Do I *really* have to be treasurer?"

"You really don't want to?"

Carlie firmly shook her head.

"I'll do it," Amy offered quickly.

"Do you want to appoint Amy to take your place?" asked Morgan.

"Can I?"

"Why don't we just vote," said Morgan. "Whoever wants Amy for treasurer, raise your hand." They all raised their hands. Morgan slapped Amy on the back. "Congratulations, Amy."

"But no speeches," warned Carlie.

"Are the sand sculptors ready to go?" asked Emily's mom as she and Kyle came out the door.

"You bet," said Morgan. "Thanks for going to work a little early today, Lisa."

"No problem," she said as she started the engine. "You want to be in time for registration ... and to make sure you get a choice piece of beach. Just yesterday I heard a couple saying that location is everything in a sand-sculpting competition." She laughed. "Although it all looks just like beach to me."

They were barely on the highway when they heard a loud bang and then a *thunkity-thunk* noise.

"Oh, no," said Kyle from the front passenger seat. "Sounds like a blowout, Mom."

Lisa pulled over on the shoulder and she and Kyle got out to see. Emily opened a window and looked out. "Is it flat?" she asked, worried that they were losing precious time now.

Her mom frowned. "Sorry, Em." She looked at Kyle. "You know how to fix a flat?"

"I guess I'm gonna learn."

"Tell the girls to get out of the van, Emily," said Mom. "On the passenger's side and stay off the road."

"We're going to be late," grumbled Amy as they climbed out of the van and went to the side of the road.

"There's nothing we can do about it," said Morgan, as she perched on the guardrail to watch.

"I'm sorry," said Emily as she sat next to Morgan.

"It's not your fault," said Carlie. "Besides, it doesn't take long to fix a flat. I was with my dad once and he had it changed within minutes."

Unfortunately, that wasn't the case today. It took Kyle and Emily's mom a long time to even figure out where the spare tire was. And then they had to figure out how to detach the spare and put the jack together. By the time they were done and everyone was back in the van, it was getting close to nine o'clock.

"The competition will be starting in ten minutes," announced Amy.

"We know," said Morgan.

"Do you think we'll be disqualified?" Emily asked her mom.

"I'll do everything I can to make sure you're not," said Mom as she drove down the highway. "But there's probably nothing we can do about the lost time."

It was a few minutes past nine when they arrived. Lisa hurried the girls to the registration area and they quickly got a number and an assigned spot on the beach.

"It's clear down at the south end of the competition," the man told them. "If you have a car, you might want to drive to save time."

"I'll drive you," said Lisa. "Kyle, go ahead and clock in. Tell Shelly that I'll be a few minutes late."

Then Lisa quickly drove the girls to the south end of the resort and pointed out where their spot should be. "Good luck," she called as they filed out of the van. "You sure you're okay for a ride home?"

"My sister An is picking us up," yelled Amy as they grabbed up their stuff and ran across the parking lot toward the beach.

"Look," said Morgan, breathlessly pointing to a sign just ahead. "There's number fifty-seven right there. We're number fifty-eight so this must be right."

"It's 9:13," announced Amy.

"We've only lost thirteen minutes," said Morgan brightly as she went for a big shovel. "No big deal."

"Just remember," said Emily as she took a flat shovel, "don't get too rushed. That's when we make mistakes. Just work consistently and listen to Morgan."

So the girls got to work. And it seemed that Morgan was right: Things were going better today than they had yesterday. And by 10:30 they all started to relax a little.

"It's not so bad down here," observed Emily as she neatly squared one of SpongeBob's corners. "We don't have a lot of foot traffic to distract us."

"Hopefully they'll come down eventually," said Amy as she worked on the crab. "I'd hate to do all this work for nothing."

"As long as the judges come," said Morgan, "that's what matters."

Carlie poured another bucket of sea water in their wet-sand area. Her job was to make sure they had just the right consistency to make the sculpture hold together. "I heard a guy talking when I was getting water," she told them. "He said there's this totally awesome sculpture of an elephant down by the restaurant."

"A standing elephant?" asked Morgan.

"Yeah. And he said there's going to be a monkey on top."

"Oh, dear," said Amy. "That doesn't sound good for us."

"It'll be fun to see it," said Morgan.

"Yeah," agreed Emily. "I can't wait to see what the others have done."

"You won't have to wait too long," warned Amy. "We have exactly seventeen minutes left."

Emily stepped back to look and smiled. Their sculpture might not beat an elephant with a monkey on top, but it was definitely good.

"Hey, that's pretty cool," called a guy's voice from behind her. She turned to see Jeff Sanders and Enrico Valdez from Derrick Smith's bunch of bullies walking up.

"Don't look now," Emily told Morgan and the others, "but trouble's heading this way."

Morgan looked up from where she was working on the snail and frowned. "Just what we need."

"You keep working," said Emily. "We'll handle this." She grabbed Carlie and walked over to stand between the guys and their sculpture.

"What do you guys want?" Emily asked the two boys.

"Hey, we're not here to make trouble," said Jeff, holding his hands up in the air as if to prove his innocence. He turned to his friend. "Right, Enrico?"

Enrico nodded innocently.

"So what are you here for then?" asked Carlie.

"We're just looking around," said Enrico.

"Yeah," said Jeff. "And it looks like you guys are making an awesome sculpture. Can we get a closer look?"

"I don't know," said Emily. "I'm not sure we can trust you guys."

"Yeah," admitted Jeff. "We can't really blame you for that."

"Really?" Emily studied the boys.

"We're done with Derrick," said Enrico. "He's definitely bad news."

"It's true," said Jeff. "Derrick's a moron."

"Why should we believe you?" asked Emily.

"Yeah," echoed Carlie. "How do we know you're not trying to trick us?" She glanced over her shoulder. "And right now you're wasting our precious time since we only have a few minutes to finish."

"Hey, sorry," said Jeff. "Don't let us keep you from finishing. It looks like you guys might actually have a chance to win something."

"Really?"

"Yeah, and to prove it, we'll get out of here. No hard feelings, okay?"

"Okay," said Emily tentatively.

The boys turned and headed back up the beach, and Emily and Carlie raced back to what they'd been doing before.

"That was weird," said Morgan. She looked up from applying some finishing touches to SpongeBob's face.

"Do you think they meant it?" asked Carlie. "That they're finished with Derrick?"

"I hope so," said Emily. She glanced up the beach. The boys were nearly out of sight.

Finally they heard the blow horn going off, their sign that the competition was over.

All four girls stepped away from the sculpture now and looked at their finished product.

"It looks pretty good," admitted Morgan with a grin.

"Better than pretty good," said Emily. "It's awesome."

"It's excellent," said Amy. "Maybe it won't beat that elephant, but it's definitely going to place second." She closed her eyes. "Let's see, three hundred divided by four would be seventy-five dollars apiece."

"As my grandma would say," said Morgan. "Don't count your chickens before they hatch, Amy."

"I'm going to take some photos of it," announced Carlie as she pulled her camera out of her beach bag. She proceeded to shoot it from several angles and even took a few shots with the girls hamming it up.

"Anybody hungry?" asked Emily as she opened the cooler and peeked inside. "Morgan's grandma put together quite a spread here."

"I'm starving," said Morgan, and all four girls attacked the cooler.

As they sat near their sculpture eating and resting, more and more spectators came their way, commenting on and praising their work. The girls thanked them, and their hopes began to get higher and higher.

"I want to go see the competition," said Morgan as she finished her last drink of soda. She stood and brushed sand from her behind. "Anyone else?" She started walking up the beach.

"I'm coming," yelled Emily.

"Me too," said Carlie.

"Don't leave me out," called Amy as she ran to catch up with them.

So they began what they agreed would be a quick walk up and down the beach to see what the other sculptors had created. And soon they began to see that competition was actually quite fierce.

"Wow," said Morgan when they were finally standing in front of the life-sized elephant who really did have a monkey on his back. "Not only is it huge, but it's got personality too."

"How did they do that?" asked Emily in amazement.

"Look," said Carlie, pointing off behind it. "They have ladders and everything."

"They'll get first place," said Amy sadly.

"We better get back to our sculpture," said Emily. "Before the judges do."

So the girls hurried back, noticing a group of what they were certain were judges only about six sites from theirs. But when they reached their site, they all froze and looked at it in horror.

"Where is SpongeBob SquarePants?" asked Amy in a small voice. They all stood by the sign for site fifty-eight. Their tools were there along with their cooler and beach stuff, but their sculpture had been completely demolished.

"Those boys!" yelled Emily. Carlie began screaming something in Spanish, shaking her fists as she did. Amy looked like she was about to cry. And Morgan collapsed onto her knees on the beach, bending over and pounding into the sand. "All our hard work!" she cried. "All for nothing!"

"What's going on here?" asked a woman's voice from behind them.

They all turned to see a group of six adults standing around their site holding clipboards and cameras and looking on with puzzled faces.

"We *had* a sculpture," began Emily in a shaky voice. "It was really awesome too." She pointed to Morgan who was still on her knees in the sand. "She designed it."

"But everyone helped," said Morgan, slowly standing. Emily could see tracks of tears down her friend's cheeks and it made Emily feel like she was about to cry too.

"It was really amazing," said Amy. "We thought it had a chance."

"But what happened?" asked a man in a Hawaiian shirt.

"We went up the beach to look around," explained Morgan. "Just for a few minutes … and while we were gone someone totally destroyed it."

"Really?" the woman in the sundress looked skeptical.

"Really," said Carlie, running to get her beach bag. "I took photos just before we left." She pulled out her camera and held it up. "We have proof."

"Unfortunately, we can't judge proof," said a judge.

Morgan nodded. "Yeah. We understand."

"We're sorry," said a short bald man. "Maybe we can see about refunding your application fee."

The girls didn't say anything.

"Hey, what happened here?" said a man who was walking toward them with several others. "What happened to SpongeBob SquarePants?"

Morgan quickly explained their misfortune once again.

"Bummer," said the man, shaking his head. "I just brought my friends here to see it. It was really something."

"Yeah," said a woman. "Everyone on the beach is talking about it."

"You were the team who made SpongeBob SquarePants?" the man in the Hawaiian shirt asked.

"Yeah," said Emily. "That was us. We got here late and ended up with the last spot on the beach. But even coming from behind, we got it finished."

Before long about a dozen or more people came and began inquiring about the missing sand sculpture. The girls explained again and again what had happened, even telling about a certain group of bullies — without using names — that had messed with them before. And, while everyone was very sympathetic, it seemed there was nothing anyone could do. Even when Carlie offered to run and get her film developed, the judges explained that they had to see the sculpture for themselves.

"But we saw it," said a woman. "And it was really good."

Several others chimed in, but the judges said that it didn't matter. "Rules are rules," said the woman in the sundress. And slowly the crowd began to move back up the beach.

"It was nice getting their sympathy," said Emily.

"Yeah, but it would be nicer to get a prize," said Amy, and they all agreed with her.

"Well, maybe they'll refund our application fee like they said." But even as she said this, Emily knew it was a small consolation. Very small.

chapter six

The girls were just starting to gather up their sand-sculpting things when Morgan announced, "Hey, look who's coming our way!"

Emily glanced up the beach, shocked to see that Jeff and Enrico were actually walking directly toward them. All four girls stood in a line with their hands on their hips and grim expressions on their faces, as if they were prepared to face off against the pair.

"Returning to the scene of the crime?" Emily called out to the boys. She was definitely ready for a confrontation.

"Huh?" said Jeff with a bewildered expression that Emily, for one, was not buying.

"Coming back to rub it in?" asked Morgan.

"We just came to see how you girls did," said Enrico as they continued walking toward them.

"Yeah," said Jeff. "What did the judges have to say?"

"About your mess?" Morgan took a step toward the boys.

"What?" Jeff looked almost believably confused now.

So the girls stepped aside to reveal their ruined sculpture and both Jeff and Enrico looked truly shocked.

"What happened?" demanded Jeff.

"Who did this?" said Enrico.

"That's what we wanted to ask you," said Emily, staring hard at their faces.

Jeff shook his head. "*We did not do this.*" He looked at all of them, directly into their eyes. "Honest. We *didn't.*"

Enrico held up his right hand like he was taking an oath of office. "I swear we didn't do this."

"Whoever did this is a total idiot," said Jeff, kicking the sand.

"Probably a red-headed idiot," added Enrico angrily.

"Hey, we did see Derrick Smith a little while ago," said Jeff suddenly. "He was on his bike, high-tailing it across the parking lot, heading *away* from the beach."

"I'll bet he did this," said Enrico. "Man, I'm so sick of that guy."

"You guys honestly didn't have anything to do with this?" demanded Morgan.

"I promise you, we didn't," said Jeff. "Like I said earlier, we've had it with Derrick. He's certifiable. We don't need his kind of trouble."

"Did you guys see Derrick at all?" asked Enrico suddenly.

The girls admitted that they hadn't. "But we did see you guys," Emily reminded the boys, still not totally convinced of their innocence.

"Do you really think we'd come back like this if we'd done that?" asked Jeff.

Morgan shrugged.

"Well, you should believe us. We didn't do it. But we'll be on the lookout for Derrick now," said Enrico. "If we find him, we'll find out whether or not he was involved."

"A lot of good that will do us now," said Carlie as she stooped to pick up a hoe.

"Hey, you want us to beat him up for you?" asked Enrico, making a fist for her.

This actually made Carlie laugh.

"No, that's not necessary," Morgan said quickly. "As much as I'd like to hurt someone, we don't need any more violence."

"But thanks for the offer," said Emily sarcastically.

"Well, if it makes you feel any better," added Jeff, "we're sorry this happened to you girls. We thought your sculpture had a really good chance of winning a prize."

"Thanks," said Morgan. The other girls thanked them too, and then the boys left. They finished gathering up their stuff and started getting ready to leave since it was pointless to stick around. Amy had already called her sister An and told her the bad news and asked her to come get them early.

"She should be here any minute," said Amy as she began trekking away from the beach with a shovel and a bucket in hand.

The girls stood on the edge of the parking lot, waiting quietly for An. It seemed clear that they were all tired—not to mention discouraged. No one wanted to talk. After about five minutes An showed up, and they quickly loaded their stuff into the back of her Honda. No one said anything as she drove back toward town.

"Sorry about your ruined day," An said as she stopped at the red light. "Amy told me the whole sad story."

"Yeah, what a disaster," said Carlie.

"Not completely," said Morgan. "At least we made some friends today."

"Who?" An glanced curiously at Morgan.

"Well, for one thing, it was amazing how the other sculptors were really sympathetic toward us and even told us that they thought we might've had a chance to win."

"Yeah," agreed Emily. "That was pretty cool."

"And I have pictures in my camera," added Carlie. "So we can always prove how good our sculpture really was, once I get them developed that is."

"And then there was that last thing ..." Morgan continued talking to An. "With these two guys, Enrico and Jeff ... They're like a year older than us and usually just act like big, stupid bullies. But today they weren't so bad."

"And it was a relief to find out that they weren't involved," added Emily.

"At least we *think* they weren't," said Carlie.

"They were actually really nice to us," said Amy.

An laughed. "Well, they should be nice. You're cute, sweet girls, and if those boys have any sense they'll figure that out before long."

An dropped them at Harbor View, and they all gathered their things and trudged off to their own houses without saying much. Emily suspected that everyone was just as tired and discouraged as she felt. And while it was somewhat encouraging to hear Morgan's optimistic take on the whole thing, Emily still felt pretty depressed about it. It just seemed so unfair. So wrong.

But that wasn't the only thing bugging her as she came inside, locked the door, and dumped her stuff on the floor. She also felt partially to blame for the whole stupid thing. If she hadn't offered for her mom to drive them to the resort on her way to work, they might've gone with someone else, someone who wouldn't have gotten a flat tire, and consequently they would have gotten there on time. And if they'd gotten there on time, they could've gotten a better site. And, instead of being off on the end where people didn't notice what was going on, they could've been right in the center of things where no one would've been able to destroy their entry. Naturally none of her friends had mentioned this, but Emily knew it was true. And she suspected that they knew it too. They were probably all blaming her right now. She was a mess-up and a loser.

Worse than that, she was probably a jinx. She remembered how her dad once told her she was a jinx — and that she brought bad luck to people. Maybe it was true.

She took a long shower and then — exhausted from the events of the day and wanting to stop thinking about how the whole thing was all her fault — she decided to take a nap. As usual, her air mattress was partially deflated, but she didn't even care. She figured it was what she deserved. And it didn't keep her from falling fast asleep.

But when she woke up, it was with a start! Someone was pounding on her bedroom window, trying to break in. Worried that it was a burglar or an ax murderer or her dad, she ran into the bathroom and locked herself in. Okay, maybe it wasn't the smartest thing to do, but since they still had no phone in the house, it was better than nothing. She held her breath and listened intently, wondering if the intruder was still trying to get in.

"Emily!" She heard Morgan's voice yelling at her from somewhere outside. *"Are you in there? Answer me!"*

Emily quickly ran out of the bathroom to unlock the front door. "I'm over here, Morgan!" she yelled, still frightened that she might be in danger. "In front of my house!"

"Oh, there you are," said Morgan as she ran up the steps where Emily was standing. "I really wish you guys would get a phone!"

"Next week," said Emily. "Mom promised. Was that you beating on my window?"

"Yeah." Morgan leaned against the porch railing to catch her breath. "No one answered the door."

"So what's going on?" asked Emily. "Why are you running around the neighborhood and scaring people half to death?"

"I'm calling an emergency club meeting," said Morgan. "Be there in ten minutes — or else!" Then, just like that, she ran off toward her own house.

Wondering what on earth was going on, Emily went back inside, put on a sweatshirt, and quickly ran a brush through her hair. She wrote her mom a note and then headed over to the Rainbow Bus. Naturally, she was the first one there, so she sat down on the bus's steps and tried to figure out why Morgan would call an emergency meeting. Maybe they had to talk about how to handle Derrick Smith. Perhaps Morgan had decided not to let him get away with his latest attack of meanness. Maybe she planned to call the police and press charges. Of course, they didn't know for sure that it was Derrick this time, even though it did seem to have his fingerprints all over it.

"Hey, you," called Morgan as she hurried up toward the bus. She had a bag in one hand and the key to the bus in the other.

"Want some help?" asked Emily.

Morgan handed her the bag as she unlocked and opened the door.

"So, what's up?" asked Emily as they went inside.

"We have to wait for the others," said Morgan as she opened a window to let in some fresh air.

"I thought I was your right-hand girl," said Emily.

Morgan nodded. "You are. But I just want to be fair. Okay?"

Emily sank down onto the couch, folding her arms across her chest as if she were offended, but then said, "Okay."

Carlie and Amy ran up and bounded into the bus.

"What's going on?" demanded Carlie. "My dad said you called and said it was an emergency." She sat down at the dining table and looked at Morgan.

"Yeah," said Amy. "What gives, Morgan? I'm supposed to help at the restaurant tonight and I can only stay a few minutes."

"Yeah," said Carlie. "I need to get back too. I'm supposed to set the table. Besides I'm starving."

"Here," said Morgan opening the brown bag and taking out four large brownies and handing them around. "Hope this doesn't spoil your dinner."

"No way," said Carlie, taking one. "I could eat all four of those and still be hungry for supper. Man, we worked so hard today. I'll bet we burned off thousands of calories."

"That's right," said Morgan with a huge smile. "We did work hard. In fact, that's exactly why I called this emergency meeting. You see, I just got a phone call ..."

"Yeah?" said Emily, leaning forward.

"From the Boscoe Bay Resort …" Morgan continued in a mysterious voice. "Apparently, Emily's mom gave them my name and phone number."

"But why?" demanded Amy.

"Come on," said Carlie. "What gives?"

"Well, it's about the sand-sculpting contest," Morgan continued. "It seems that the committee decided to have what they call a 'People's Choice Award.'"

"What's that?" asked Carlie.

"They put out a ballot box, right there on the beach," she winked at Amy, "and probably not a Kleenex box either. And they invited everyone, including contestants and spectators, to write in the number of their favorite sand-sculpture entry. And …" Morgan paused.

"*And?*" Emily was pulling on Morgan's arm, trying to get her to quit stringing them along.

"And we won." Morgan calmly smiled at the others.

"*We won?*" said Amy.

"Yeah!" Morgan yelled the good news now. "*We won!*" And then all four girls were laughing and jumping and hugging each other, so much that the bus was actually rocking with their movements. Finally they quieted down.

"So, what did we win?" asked Carlie.

"Well, along with the ballot box, it seems they also put out another box that was for donations. The People's Choice Award gets a prize that's totally donated, and the amount given was three hundred seventy-eight dollars."

"Three hundred seventy-eight dollars?" Emily echoed in amazement.

"That's ninety-four dollars and fifty cents each," said Amy without even blinking.

"Or something like that," said Morgan, rolling her eyes.

"No, that's correct." said Amy seriously, "you can check it on a calculator." The other girls laughed.

"How much is it if we put half of the total back into the bus?" asked Emily.

Amy paused for about a second and then said, "That would be forty-seven dollars and twenty-five cents each, and then we'd have one hundred eighty-nine dolars to use for the bus."

"How does she do that?" Carlie scratched her head with a puzzled expression.

"It's a gift," said Morgan.

"I can't believe it," said Emily. "We really won the People's Choice Award?"

"It's true," said Morgan. "Oh, yeah, Carlie, the manager at the resort asked if you could get those pictures developed in time to go in Tuesday's newspaper?"

"Wow, we're going to be in the newspaper again?" said Amy. "That's twice in one month!"

"It's a small town," said Morgan.

Emily just hoped it was small enough that her dad wouldn't somehow get wind of this. Of course, she reminded herself, her dad seldom read the newspaper or watched the news. He thought it was all "a bunch of propaganda."

"No problem," said Carlie. "I'll ask dad to drop my film off at the overnight place tonight. We can have prints by tomorrow."

"This is so great," said Amy, "But I better get back before my brother decides to leave for the restaurant without me."

"Group hug first," said Morgan. And all three girls embraced for a good, tight group hug. Then she held up her arm with the rainbow bracelet on it. "Way to go, girls," she said. The others held up their bracelets too.

"Rainbows rule!" said Amy.

"Rainbows rule!" echoed the others.

"Let's meet tomorrow afternoon," said Morgan as they went out and waited for her to lock up the bus. "After church. Like two o'clock?"

"Sounds good to me," said Amy.

"Maybe my photos will be done by then," said Carlie.

Then they all said good-bye, heading their separate ways. And, as Emily went into her house, she felt a renewed sense of hope. Maybe she hadn't jinxed the group after all. Maybe with God in her life, things really were changing.

On Sunday, the girls met at two. They decided to walk to town to see if Carlie's prints were ready yet. Fortunately they were, and after carefully looking at all of them, they picked out several that looked really good. They walked over to the newspaper office only to find that it was closed.

"We'll bring them first thing tomorrow," said Morgan.

Back at the Rainbow Bus, the girls settled in, opened some windows for fresh air, and shared a bag of Oreos provided by Carlie.

"When do we get the prize money?" asked Amy.

"The guy at the hotel said we can pick it up on Monday. He wants us all to come so we can get our picture taken."

"Maybe we can just give him one of these," said Carlie, holding up the packet of photos.

"My mom could give us a ride to the resort," said Emily. "But then she couldn't bring us home."

"And it's a long walk," said Carlie.

"I'll ask Grandma to drive us," said Morgan.

"Should we decide how we want to use our prize money for the bus?" asked Amy, setting the notebook on the table like she was ready to start writing things down.

"I thought I was the secretary," said Emily, sliding the notebook over to herself.

"Is this an official meeting?" asked Morgan.

"I don't know, Madam President," said Amy. "Is it?"

Morgan shrugged. "Why not?"

"Are you going to call the meeting to order?" asked Amy.

"Okay," said Morgan in an even voice. "I realize that you like to do things your way, Amy, but since I'm president, I get to run the meeting my way. And I'm not into all that fancy-schmancy meeting rules stuff. I mean, it's fine for Emily to take notes, if she wants to and needs to, and you can do whatever you think a treasurer should do. But I am a free spirit and I refuse to be put in a box."

"Amen!" said Emily, stifling a giggle.

Morgan laughed. "You sound just like Walter Alpenheimer."

"Who's Walter Alpenheimer?" asked Amy.

"This guy at church who always says 'Amen' after everything."

"Amen," said Emily again.

"So, am I clear?" asked Morgan.

"Works for me," said Carlie.

"Whatever," said Amy.

"Okay," began Morgan. "For starters, I would like to see us get some kind of new covering for that sorry old couch." She pointed to the faded and frayed fabric where some of the stuffing was starting to come out. "I mean, we cleaned and scrubbed it the best we could, and that blanket from my house sort of covers it up. But I think we could do better."

"I agree," said Emily.

"Me too," said Carlie.

"How much do you think that will cost?" asked Amy.

Morgan considered this. "I don't know. But we'll get the best deal we can. And while I'm on that subject, I'd like something nicer to cover the bed with too. That mattress is kind of gross and the blanket sort of works, but you know how it slips off. I'd like to do something that makes it prettier and more comfortable. And we need more pillows, you know, so we can lean back there and read and stuff."

Once again, everyone agreed.

"But how much will it cost?" demanded Amy.

"I don't know," Morgan said again. "Do you want to come with me to the fabric store?"

"Why don't we all go?" suggested Carlie.

So it was agreed. After picking up the prize money and dropping off the photos, they would ask Grandma to take them to the fabric store.

"Do you think she'll mind?" asked Emily.

Morgan laughed. "It's a fabric store! She loves those places."

So on Monday they all met at Morgan's house, and Grandma drove them around to do their errands. They made their final stop the fabric store, which happened to be having a big clearance sale. To everyone's relief, they found some great deals on fabric. After several discussions — and near arguments — about color, pattern, and style, they agreed that bright was better and selected a hot pink and orange zebra-striped plush fabric for both the couch and the bed. Amy was the only one with reservations about the bright colors, but even she seemed to be coming around as they picked out some fun prints for pillows.

"I guess I am a little conservative about color," she admitted after everything was laid out in the bus. "I have to admit that this does really perk the place up."

"And just think how good it will feel in here on some gray, foggy day," Morgan pointed out.

"And there are plenty of those," agreed Amy.

Then Morgan put everyone to work on a different part of the sewing project. And by the end of the day, they had both the bed and the couch covered with the new fabric.

"This feels so good," said Amy as the four of them sprawled across the plush-covered bed. "It's like sleeping on a teddy bear."

"Well, I think that was a good accomplishment for today," said Morgan. "We'll work on the pillows tomorrow — maybe even finish up all the sewing completely — and then I have something special planned for Wednesday and Thursday."

"What?" asked Emily.

"An art project," said Morgan. "Something to brighten up the walls."

"How much will it cost?" asked Amy. "You know we only have forty-eight dollars and seventy-four cents left in our bus fund. And we need to keep some in reserves."

"Reserves?" said Emily.

"Yes. In case of emergencies."

"What kind of emergencies?" asked Carlie.

"You think we might get a flat tire?" teased Morgan.

"Or blow out our engine?" added Emily.

Amy rolled her eyes. "Something could come up. As treasurer, I recommend we keep at least $20 in our reserves. And I think we should consider having monthly fees."

"Is this a business meeting?" asked Morgan, sitting up on the bed and looking at Amy.

"Well, no …"

Morgan flopped back down. "Good."

"But you did say that you like doing things differently," Amy reminded her. "So maybe it's okay to have a business meeting while we're lying down on the bed."

"Fine," said Morgan. "Might as well get it over with. Just so you know, I think keeping some money in our reserves is probably a good idea. And $20 is plenty. But I'm not sure about monthly dues. Although I do think we could come up with ways to earn money if we decided we needed it. I just don't want that to be the main focus of our club." She held up her bracelet. "It's more about friendship, you know."

"I agree," said Emily, relieved that she wouldn't be pressured to come up with ways to pay her monthly dues. As it was, she didn't even have an allowance yet.

"Me too," said Carlie. "Now tell us about the art project, Morgan."

"All I'll say now is that it's going to involve paint." Morgan sighed. "And now for the bad news."

"Bad news?" said Emily, sitting up. The other girls sat up too. Only Morgan remained in a reclined position, a sad expression over her face.

"What bad news?" asked Amy.

"Yeah, out with it," said Carlie. "What's going on?"

"Well, it's funny because I would've considered this good news last summer. In fact, I remember begging my mom for this exact thing."

"What?" demanded Emily as she pulled Morgan up to a sitting position.

"Yeah, quit stringing us along," said Carlie.

"Okay. My mom goes to this big trade show every summer for people who run gift shops or tourist shops or whatever. Anyway, she always comes home with lots of cool free stuff, and it always sounded so fun, and I always used to ask her if I could go. And now she invites me."

"What's so bad about that?" asked Emily.

"I'll be gone for most of a week," said Morgan sadly. "And we've been having so much fun hanging together, and the clubhouse is almost all fixed up, and …" She flopped back down again. "I'll miss out on all the fun."

"When do you go?" asked Emily.

"Next week." Morgan groaned. "Mom gave me my airline ticket as an early birthday present. There's no backing out now."

"When's your birthday?" asked Amy.

"July thirteenth."

"Oh."

"So you'll be thirteen on the thirteenth?" said Amy.

"Yeah, I guess so."

"Where's the trade show?" asked Emily.

"All the way in Atlanta, Georgia." Morgan just shook her head.

"I think it sounds pretty fun," admitted Emily.

"And glamorous," added Carlie.

"And you get free stuff?" said Amy.

Morgan sat up now and smiled. "But I'll miss you guys so much."

"We'll miss you too," said Emily. "But I'll bet you'll have lots of fun."

"Besides," Amy slapped her forehead. "I almost forgot … I have music camp next week."

"Music camp?" Morgan frowned. "What is that?"

"It's a camp that focuses on music," said Amy. "Like, duh."

"So you go there and play music?" asked Emily.

"Something like that. You'd have to be into music like I am to fully appreciate it."

Morgan laughed. "In other words, a music geek."

"Hey," said Amy.

"Sorry," said Morgan. "You're not a music geek, Amy. I was just kidding."

"Well, it's kind of true," admitted Amy. "I know I'm a geek. Other kids have been telling me that for years now."

"You are not a geek," said Emily.

"You're just a little uptight sometimes," said Carlie.

"Yeah," said Morgan. "You do need to loosen up, Amy." She laughed as she poked Amy in the ribs. "That's probably why God gave you us."

"Yeah," said Carlie as they all started tickling Amy. "To loosen you up." Then Amy was laughing so loudly that she made a hilarious snorting sound. That got them all laughing so hard that they actually had tears coming down their cheeks.

"Stop! Stop!" laughed Amy, even though the tickling had ended several minutes ago. "Or I'm going to burst."

Finally it quieted down.

"So Amy and I will both be gone," said Morgan. "What are you guys going to do without us?"

"Actually," said Carlie. "It's the Fourth of July this weekend, isn't it?"

"Yeah," said Morgan. "Why?"

"I kind of forgot that I promised my mom I'd watch the boys while she and Tia Maria take a bookkeeping class at the community college. And I just remembered that the class was supposed to be the week after the Fourth of July."

Morgan turned to Emily. "So, let me guess. You're probably going somewhere too?"

Emily just shook her head. "Nope. I'll be here."

Morgan nodded. "Well, then you can look after things for us. I'll put you officially in charge of the bus."

Emily forced a smile. "Gee, thanks."

"Speaking of the Fourth of July," said Morgan. "Anybody got plans?"

"I plan to watch the fireworks." Amy rolled her eyes. "Just like always."

"Yeah," said Morgan. "Did you guys know that you can see the fireworks from right here?"

"Yeah, big deal," said Amy. "Everyone in Harbor View drags out their lawn chairs, sits around watching the big show, and then goes to bed."

"Or you can watch it from the beach," suggested Morgan.

"I think that sounds like fun," said Carlie.

"Maybe we should make it even more fun," said Morgan. "We could invite all the neighbors down for a hot dog roast on the beach, have a big campfire, and then watch the fireworks from there."

"That sounds pretty good," said Amy.

"I think it sounds great," agreed Carlie.

"Maybe it could be a potluck," said Morgan. "I'll see if my grandma wants to help organize it."

And suddenly they were all talking about the Fourth of July. Everyone except for Emily. All she could think about was that she had one whole week of being on her own. What would she do?

chapter eight

The girls, along with the other winners of the First Annual Boscoe Bay Resort Sandcastle-Building Contest, made the front page of Tuesday's newspaper.

"Look at this," said Amy as she read the part about how the girls had won "'despite the mean-spirited sabotage of their artwork.'"

"They called SpongeBob SquarePants *artwork!*" said Amy.

"It *was* artwork," insisted Morgan as she tossed a finished pillow at Amy's head. The girls were working in the Rainbow Bus stuffing and sewing pillows closed.

Amy said, "Listen to this!"

"Are you still reading the paper?" said Morgan. "You're supposed to be sewing, Amy."

"I needed a break." Amy frowned at her. "Now listen to what I just read on page three. *Vandals Strike Washington Elementary. Late Sunday night, juvenile vandals spray-painted graffiti and profanity on parts of Washington Elementary. Also, some windows were broken. According to school officials, the building was not entered. Estimate of property damage is listed at about $2,500.00. A minor has been* taken into custody for questioning. Police say that spray-paint cans found at the scene may link this crime to a similar act of vandalism that occurred at Harbor View Mobile-Home Court a few weeks ago.'"

"Wow, do you think they caught Derrick Smith?" asked Emily.

"It definitely sounds like they caught the person who destroyed all our hard work cleaning up the trailer park this spring," said Morgan.

By Friday, the girls had completely finished redecorating the inside of the Rainbow Bus. Morgan's interior painting project — geometric designs of spots and stripes and plaids — had provided the bus with just the right final touches that it needed. To celebrate, the girls invited their families and Mr. Greeley to an impromptu "bus warming" that evening after dinner. And, of course, everyone was very impressed.

"I wonder why Mr. Greeley didn't come," said Morgan as they cleaned up the paper cups and napkins afterwards. Grandma, Morgan, and Emily had prepared refreshments of punch and cookies.

"Maybe he was busy," said Carlie as she scooped cookie crumbs from the table into the garbage bag.

"Yeah, right," said Emily. "Probably had a hot date."

They laughed.

"Still, I wish he'd come see it," said Morgan. "Don't you think he'd be pleased with all we've done?"

"I don't know," said Emily as she put the leftover punch in the little fridge. "I still have the feeling that he doesn't want anything to do with the bus. Like he gave it to us just to get it off his hands." What she didn't tell them was her suspicion that there could've been some kind of foul play between Mr. Greeley and Dan Watterson. She knew it was probably just her overactive imagination, but she still didn't trust the old man.

"Whatever the reason …" said Carlie, collapsing onto their plush couch. "Aren't we glad he did?"

Morgan picked up the beaded curtain that her mom had brought the girls as a housewarming gift. "Should we hang this up here?" she said as she held it up near the front door. "To make a good entrance?"

"That looks beautiful," said Emily as she helped her attach the sticky tape to the ceiling.

"Perfect," said Carlie when they finished.

"It's all perfect," said Amy.

"Then let's call it a night," said Morgan.

"I'm glad they caught the vandal," said Emily as Morgan locked the door to the bus. "I've worried that whoever it was, whether it's Derrick or some other crazy person, might hit our bus."

"I had the same thought," admitted Amy.

"Me too," said Morgan. "I actually pray that God will protect our bus."

"That's a good idea," said Emily.

"Yeah," agreed Carlie as she bent down to pinch a dead leaf off the pot of geraniums that she'd set by the bus door. "Maybe we should do some kind of bus blessing. I've been to house blessings before. You know, when someone moves into a new place, they get their friends to come and bless it. Kind of like our bus warming tonight."

"Good idea," said Morgan. "Maybe we should do it right now."

So the four girls stood outside while Morgan led them in a prayer for the bus, asking God to keep it safe and to make it a happy place for them to hang out together. Then she stopped. "Anyone else want to pray?" So Emily thanked God for giving them the bus as well as their friendships, and she asked God to bless their club.

"Anyone else?" asked Morgan.

So now Carlie prayed, mostly repeating what Morgan and Emily had said, but it sounded sincere.

Morgan glanced at Amy. "You want to add anything?"

Amy just shrugged. "I think that was good. Besides I don't really know how to pray."

"Well, you're going to have to learn," said Morgan.

"Yeah," agreed Emily. "It's not hard. It's just talking to God."

On Saturday night, most of the neighbors of Harbor View Mobile-Home Court trekked down to the beach for a hot dog roast, potluck, and fireworks. And when it was all over with, Amy admitted that it was the best Fourth of July in their neighborhood — ever.

And even though Emily had lived there less than two months, she had to agree.

On Sunday, Morgan handed the bus key over to Emily. And by Monday, everyone seemed to have left town.

Of course, Carlie was still around. But Emily knew that Carlie would have her hands full with her two little brothers. And so Emily would be mostly on her own.

On Monday, Emily slowly walked over to the bus. No reason to hurry since no one would be there today — or anytime this week. It was foggy and chilly this morning and Emily wished she'd put on long pants instead of her thin, cotton shorts. But she remembered that Carlie's dad had recently tested out the little heater to make sure that it was safe. She might be lonely, but she didn't have to be cold. As soon as she was inside and had locked the door (Morgan's recommendation for any of the girls who were in the bus alone), she turned on the heater and just walked around. Morgan had been right about the bright colors. They did make the place feel warm and cheerful on a gray day. Even so, Emily knew it would be much warmer and cheerier if her friends were here. Even Amy, who could be cantankerous sometimes, would be an improvement over this solitude.

"Get over it," she said aloud as she walked to the back of the bus, trying to decide what to do. Then she remembered the box of books that was still underneath the bed. With all their recent activities, she had nearly forgotten it. And now would be a good time to sort and place the books up on the empty bookshelf over the bed. Plus the books would make the place look even better — more lived in. So she removed all the pillows and lifted up the mattress. And there, not only was the box of books, but also the record albums and the record player that they hadn't even tried out yet.

"No time like now," she said as she removed all the items and finally closed the bed and replaced the pillows. First, she took the record player up to the front of the bus. She set it on the passenger seat, near an electrical outlet, and plugged it in. Remembering Mr. Garcia's warning about not running too much electricity at once, she turned off the heater before turning on the record player. To her pleased surprise, it worked.

She went back for the apple crate of old vinyl records, placing it on the floor near the dashboard. Then she began to flip through the records, wondering which one to start with. Finally she decided on Elton John. At least she knew who that was. She slipped the big, black vinyl disk out of the cardboard album jacket, carefully placed it on the turntable, and turned it on. There was a switch with three numbers — 78, 45, and 33. She had no idea what they were for, but remembered hearing Morgan calling these records 33s, so she switched it to that. Then she lifted up the arm and set it to rest on the turning record, and suddenly there was quiet music coming out. She turned the volume up and went to the couch to sit and listen. Very nice. She decided that she liked Elton John.

She left the music playing and started to put books on the shelf. Suddenly it occurred to her that this was kind of nice. She had good music, interesting books, and a cool place to hang out. And it was kind of a relief having it quiet in here for a change. Like it gave her time to think. Plus, with no one chattering away or looking over her shoulder, she could really check out the books as she placed them, one by one, on the shelf. She took her time to open the mysteries, read the first few lines, and decide which one she might like to read first. She noticed that Dan Watterson's name was written in some of the books and, once again, she wondered about this guy. Who he was? And what had been his connection to this bus?

As she was getting the books arranged, she pulled out the old high school yearbook again. She flipped around to the pages that had pictures of Dan Watterson. She noticed that he was most often pictured with a girl with long, dark hair. Finally Emily found the girl's name by a photo of the two of them in formal attire. Stephanie Chetwood.

She looked up the girl in the senior section, but found she wasn't there. So she looked in the junior section and, sure enough, there was Stephanie Chetwood. So she had been a year younger than Dan. Emily thought the girl was really pretty — even by today's standards. She had big, dark eyes and straight, dark hair.

Emily looked back through the handwritten notes in the yearbook, hoping to find what Stephanie had said about Dan. And there, tucked two pages from the back was a very tiny note, written in very small handwriting that had faded a bit with time. Emily squinted to read it. "'To Dan, the love of my life, your Steph.'"

"Wow," said Emily as she read it again. "The love of his life." She closed the book and wondered if they might've gotten married. Maybe Dan graduated and went to college. And maybe Steph did too, and then maybe they got married and had kids. Hey, it was possible that they could actually live in town. Right here in Boscoe Bay! What Emily needed was a phone book. And since they'd just gotten their phone last week, she knew just where to find one.

She turned off the record player, locked the bus, and dashed home to check their new phone book. But there was no Dan Watterson listed. In fact, no one by that last name was listed. She closed the book and sighed. There must be some way to find out this guy's whereabouts. She wished she was brave enough to ask Mr. Greeley, but since he hadn't come to their bus-warming party, and no one had seen him at the Fourth of July hot dog roast, she got the feeling that he was lying low and not wishing for company.

Emily wondered about Morgan's grandma. She knew that Grandma had only lived in Harbor View for the last ten years, after she had retired from teaching high school in another town. It seemed unlikely that she would know. Besides, knowing Morgan, she'd probably already asked. Then Emily remembered Mrs. Hardwick and her son who worked at the newspaper. She seemed to know a lot of people. And she was friendly too. Maybe Emily could ask her. But first she put on her jeans and a sweatshirt. Then she tucked an apple and granola bar into her big front pocket for lunch and took off, heading for Mrs. Hardwick's for a quick visit.

"Sorry to disturb you," she said when the older woman came to the door.

"Not at all," said the woman. "You're Emily, right?"

She nodded. "I don't want to take too much of your time, but I'm curious if you've lived here very long."

"In Harbor View Mobile-Home Court?" asked the woman.

"Yes."

"Goodness, it's been … let's see … I think about twenty-five years. Or thereabouts."

"Wow, that's a long time," said Emily.

Mrs. Hardwick laughed. "Well, for a young person, I suppose it seems that way. I was about fifty when I moved here from Ridgeport. My husband had just passed and I didn't like living in a big old house by myself."

Emily nodded. "Did you ever know a man named Dan Watterson?"

Mrs. Hardwick frowned. "The name doesn't sound familiar. Did he live here?"

"Maybe."

"Well, I think I've lived in the court longer than anyone — other than Mr. Greeley."

"How long has he been here?" asked Emily, suddenly wishing she'd thought to write out some questions.

"Well, he started up the place. And it was still pretty new when I moved in here. Only about five or six other mobile homes had been set in place at the time. But I think it had been running for a few years by then." She looked carefully at Emily. "Are you girls working on some new kind of project now? Writing up the history of the place?"

"Not exactly," said Emily. "We're just curious."

Mrs. Hardwick smiled. "Well, that's nice. It's refreshing to see some kids taking an interest in something besides their fancy computers and televisions."

Emily smiled. "Thanks. I better go now."

The old woman waved as Emily walked away. She tried not to laugh about the "fancy computer" comment.

Emily hadn't had a computer to use for nearly two months now. And they'd only gotten their hand-me-down TV a week ago. And since they didn't even have cable, it wasn't too tempting to turn into a couch potato. Still, Mrs. Hardwick's computer comment gave Emily an idea. And instead of returning to the bus, Emily headed to town. It was about an eight-minute walk from the trailer park, six if you walked fast. She took her time and ate her apple and granola bar along the way.

Emily had seen the public library from the street, but up until now she hadn't been inside. It was a small building with the same musty book smell that all libraries seemed to have. Emily stopped at the front desk and asked the small, white-haired lady about computers.

"We have four set up right over by the window for public use," said the woman.

"Do you have to have a library card?" asked Emily.

"No, anyone can use them, dear. Just read the rules posted there and be courteous to other patrons."

Emily thanked her and said, "As long as I'm here, may I have an application for a library card? I actually do like to read too."

The woman smiled as she handed her a yellow piece of paper. "Then you came to the right place."

So Emily took the application and went over to the computer section where she logged in and then tried several different searches on the name "Daniel Watterson." The first search, with only his name, provided so many references that it would take her a lifetime to read them all, so she decided to narrow it down by trying his name along with "Boscoe Bay News." This resulted in several old sports stories about the Boscoe Bay Cougars and Dan's athletic contributions during his high school career. There were also many references to college scholarships. So she decided to try those. Unfortunately the ones she attempted to trace seemed to have nothing to do with her Dan Watterson. Finally she gave up.

Before leaving, Emily filled out the library card application and took it back to the woman at the front desk. She felt a little bit guilty for using the name Adams, but she knew that it was for her family's own safety. Her dad might trace down their family here if she used her real name.

"Are you new here?" asked the woman as she glanced down over the application.

"Yes. We've only been here a couple of months."

The woman smiled. "Well, a library card can be a good friend when you're new in town."

Emily was about to tell the woman that even though she was new in town, she did have friends — good friends too. But she decided that might sound rude. Instead she thanked her.

"Did you wish to check out any books today?"

"No. I have a book that I'm about to start. It's a mystery."

The woman nodded. "Oh, I do love a good mystery. And we have lots of them here."

"Then I'll definitely be back," said Emily. She looked up at the clock on the wall behind the woman and was surprised to see that it was already 4:45, and today was a day when Mom and Kyle got home at five. She'd have to hurry to make it home before them. As she jogged home, she realized that her first day without friends around had passed fairly quickly. Now if only the rest of the week would go this fast.

At dinner, Emily asked her mom about Mr. Greeley. "Don't you think he's kind of weird?" she said after mentioning how he never came to anything social.

"I think he's just sad," said Mom.

"I think he's creepy," said Kyle. "Did you see how long the hair growing out of his ears is? Hey, maybe he's a werewolf."

"Kyle!" Mom glared at him.

"Well, he is strange, Mom," pointed out Emily.

"All I know is he was good to us. When we came here, I didn't have enough money for rent," Mom told them. "He assured me it was okay. He said he understood how people have hard times. And he was very understanding."

"He probably thinks you're hot," said Kyle.

"Kyle!" Mom looked really angry now.

"Sorry."

"Well, you kids be nice to him. He's been good to us. I don't know where we would be if he hadn't been willing to rent this place to me. He's a good-hearted man. Even when I gave him our real name — so he could do a credit check — he promised me that he would keep it secret. And I have no reason not to trust him."

Emily wasn't so sure about that, but she figured if Mom trusted him, maybe she should too. Still, she would keep a safe distance for now!

chapter nine

On Tuesday, Emily returned to the bus with a mission: She would do all she could to figure out who Dan Watterson was. And if she came up with nothing, she would put the case to rest. No sense in making herself crazy over some old dude who happened to leave his high school yearbook in somebody's old bus.

She turned on the record player again, this time turning the Elton John album to the other side, and then she went to the back of the bus to finish putting the books on the shelf. But when she got to the bottom of the box, she saw a small, black book that she hadn't noticed before. She pulled it out to discover it was a journal. And it had been written in. There was no name inside of it, but when she compared the handwriting to the books with Dan Watterson's name written in them, it appeared to be the same. A very neat and angular style that looked more like printing than cursive.

Feeling slightly intrusive, but curious, Emily began to read. And she was thankful — not for the first time — that the other girls weren't around. Not that she planned to hide this from them, but she hated the idea of them making fun of this guy. Emily knew what it was like to keep a journal. She'd been doing so for years. But nothing would humiliate her more as a writer than if someone found her personal thoughts and hopes and dreams and made fun of them. That's why she'd always kept her journals well hidden. It still bothered her deeply that they'd left so quickly that night, she had left a few journals behind. She hoped and prayed her dad never found them.

As Emily read, she felt she could relate to Dan Watterson. He too loved words and aspired to be a writer. He had a column in the school paper, and despite having the image of a jock, he'd secretly written poetry. A lot of poetry. Who would've guessed? She also learned that he did get a sports scholarship to Oregon State, but that he dropped out of college before graduating. And the reason he dropped out was because of a girl. She came to this conclusion since the thing he wrote about most in his journal was Stephanie, his high school sweetheart. It seemed that his devotion was as strong as hers, and that she was the love of his life. But for some reason she had disappeared — left his life without a trace. And as a result, he was lost and heartbroken and devoted many poems to her.

Finally, Emily closed the journal. The last dozen entries were spread out over several years, written from all over the country, but they still sounded very unhappy. As soon as she set the book aside she felt horribly guilty, like she had sneaked into someone's private world. And even though she was still curious, and her desire to solve this Dan the man mystery was strong, she knew she must not go back and reread a single sentence. She also knew that it would be wrong for the other girls to read it too. In fact, she was tempted to destroy the journal altogether. But that seemed wrong too.

Eventually, she decided to find a really good hiding place for it — a place on the bus because it belonged with the bus. The other important thing that Emily learned from the journal was that this had indeed been Dan's bus. He'd bought it from a friend named Jim shortly after he dropped out of college. And even though his dad was furious with him, he lived in this bus, drove around the country, and seemed to have no idea what he would do with his life.

Emily walked around the bus, searching for a safe spot to hide the sad journal. After a thorough search she decided to shove it behind a loose board in the little closet near the bedroom. She felt it would be safe there. As far as Dan went, maybe she would never know anything else. Maybe it was none of her business. But this journal was a private thing and she would respect that.

On Wednesday and Thursday, Emily tried to put thoughts of Dan Watterson behind her as she immersed herself in reading mysteries and writing some poetry of her own. But the more time she spent in the bus, the more

she felt that Dan was there too ... and the more she felt
that this mystery was not going to leave her alone until
she had resolved it. So she opened up her own journal
and began to write down the questions that seemed to be
nagging the loudest.

1. Why is Dan's bus parked at Harbor View?
2. Where is Dan now?
3. What is his relationship to Mr. Greeley?
4. What happened to Stephanie?

And that was about it. Not too difficult, really. Emily
scratched her head as she stared at these four questions.
It seemed the only way she'd find the answers would be
to approach Mr. Greeley. And yet that scared the socks
off her.

So she paused and asked herself: *How else do people
research these things? What do people in the mystery books
do?* She'd already tried the computer without success. This
reminded her of the sweet, white-haired librarian, and she
wondered, *How long had that woman lived in town?* She
might be more helpful than a computer. Besides, she told
herself as she walked toward town, she'd soon be out of
mysteries. She might as well restock her supply. Hopefully
that same librarian would be there again.

Sure enough, the white-haired woman was there. And
to Emily's surprise, she even seemed to recognize her.

"Ready for a mystery?" asked the woman when Emily
paused in front of her big shiny desk.

"Sort of …" Emily smiled. "Actually, I'm trying to solve a mystery."

"To solve one?" The woman looked curious.

"And I thought maybe you could help me."

"Me?"

"Yes. That is if you've lived in Boscoe Bay for very long. Have you?"

She laughed. "Well, that depends on how you look at it. It doesn't seem that long to me, but I was born and raised here, and I've lived here all my life."

Emily smiled. "So maybe you can help me. I'm trying to find out about someone. You see I have something that belongs to him — actually a few things — that I found in a box. And I think they might be valuable to him because they're memorabilia. You know what I mean?"

She nodded. "Yes. I can understand that. Who is it you're looking for, dear?"

"Daniel Watterson."

The woman nodded with a creased brow as if trying to remember.

"Do you know him?" Emily asked hopefully.

"I did know him."

"You did?" Emily wanted to jump for joy but — remembering this was a library — controlled herself.

"I used to teach English at the high school. Dan was one of my students. A very bright boy. Popular too. And very good at sports. So much potential …" Her face grew sad.

"Do you know where he is?" asked Emily. "Does he live around here?"

"Dan died in the Middle East."

"Huh?" Emily frowned at her. "In the Iraq War?"

"No, dear, it was Desert Storm."

"Desert Storm?"

"Do they teach about that in history yet?"

"Not exactly."

"Well, that war was in 1991 and didn't last long. I believe Dan was several years out of college when he went over. I remember being surprised that he'd joined up." She sighed. "And he was one of the unfortunate few who never came back."

"Oh," Emily didn't know what to say, but she could feel tears gathering in her eyes. "Do you mean he was killed?"

She nodded. "I'm sorry to tell you such sad news, dear."

"It's okay." Emily attempted a smile. "I mean it's not your fault. I just had no idea."

"Will you be okay, dear?"

Emily nodded, swallowing against the lump in her throat.

"I don't know what to tell you about the box of memorabilia. The Wattersons left town many years ago, not long after Dan graduated from high school, as I recall. I have no idea where they moved."

"That's okay," said Emily. All she wanted now was to get out of here. She didn't want people to see her crying. "Thanks, Mrs...."

The woman extended her hand. "Mrs. Drimmel," she said.

"Emily Adams." She blinked back tears.

"You take care now," said Mrs. Drimmel. "And next time you come in, I'll show you some good mysteries."

"Thanks." Emily hurried out, trying to hold back the tears as she walked quickly through town. She didn't know why she was taking this so hard, except that it was as if Dan had become a personal friend this week. It was so shocking, so sad, to hear that he was dead. Finally, worried that she might see someone, or someone might see her, Emily began jogging toward home. But instead of going into her house, she went straight to the Rainbow Bus. Then she went inside and locked the door, and she turned on the record player — turned it up loud and just cried.

Finally, after a few minutes, Emily stopped crying. The music was still playing, the same Elton John album that she'd had on just the other day. But this time, as a certain song came on, she listened carefully to the lyrics. The song was about a man, also named Daniel, who was leaving on a plane. He'd had a lot of pain, and now it was time to say good-bye. Emily cried when it came to the line about how Daniel's eyes had died. And then she kept singing the last line: "must be the clouds in my eyes."

The song ended and she turned off the record player. And then she sat down in the driver's seat of the bus and began to pray. "Dear God," she said with her eyes wide open, looking out over the dunes to where she knew the Harbor was. "I know I never really knew Dan Watterson personally, but it feels like I did. And his story is so sad. So very, very sad. Is there anything I can do to help? Or should I just let this thing go? Should I wave good-bye to Daniel and try to forget about it? Please, dear God, show me what to do. Amen."

Then she noticed someone walking along the beach road. At first she felt scared, imagining that she'd just seen Dan's ghost. But then she realized it was only Mr. Greeley. But as she watched him, slowly walking along with his head hanging low, she felt bad. She realized how wrong it was to be suspicious of him — thinking he'd done something to Dan Watterson when he was completely innocent.

She opened the window on the driver's side and called out. "Mr. Greeley?"

He turned to see who it was, then gave her a small halfhearted wave.

"How's it going?" she yelled out the window.

"All right."

Then, without even questioning herself, she hurried outside and ran over to join him. "You taking a walk?" she asked.

"Yep."

"Can I come too?"

He peered curiously at her. "I reckon."

"Going to the beach?" she asked as they began walking.

"Yep."

"Kind of foggy today," she said, wishing for something better to say.

"Yep."

"And cold too."

"Yep."

"We really like our bus, Mr. Greeley."

He turned and looked at her, almost smiling now. "That's good."

"We fixed it all up inside. You should come see it sometime."

He nodded without saying anything, and they just walked in silence for a couple of minutes. Emily was starting to get worried, wondering what on earth she was doing. Why had she come down to the beach with this old guy who she only recently suspected of murder?

"We found some things while we were fixing the bus up ..." she said as they walked toward the Harbor.

He stopped walking. "What kinds of things?"

She stopped walking too. "Personal things."

He frowned. "I took everything off that bus."

"Well, a bunch of things were stored under the bed."

"*Under* the bed?" He looked skeptical.

"Yeah. There's this kind of secret storage spot there. We found books and record albums and—"

"You said *personal* things?"

"That's right." She studied his face. "Did you know Dan Watterson, Mr. Greeley?"

He slowly nodded.

"He sounded like a really nice guy," said Emily.

"He was."

"I'm curious as to why he left his bus on your property?" she said in a gentle voice. "Was he a friend of yours?"

He nodded again, this time looking off toward the ocean.

"Well, I feel like he was my friend too," she said suddenly.

"Huh?" He looked at her.

"I feel like I know him now." She looked into Mr. Greeley's faded eyes. "This week the other girls have been gone, and I've been reading his books and listening to his music and even reading his journal ... and I feel like I really know him." She sighed. "And then I found out how he died in the war." She felt tears coming again, and she knew she wouldn't be able to stop them. "And I've been so sad. I feel like my friend just died."

He nodded, and she saw tears running down his wrinkled old cheeks too. "Yep," he said. "Me too."

"Do you want to talk about it, Mr. Greeley?" she asked.

He peered down at her, and she could almost see him thinking how she was just a kid and wondering why he should talk to her.

"I've been through some hard things too," she told him.

He nodded. "Yep, I s'pect you have."

And so they continued walking, and Mr. Greeley started to talk. And he talked and talked and talked. And finally, after all her investigating and all her wondering and searching, the whole story of Daniel Watterson unfolded. Finally she understood what had happened.

"Wow," she told him as they turned around to walk back toward the trailer court. "That must've been so hard."

He nodded. "Yep."

"Do you think you'd want to read Dan's journal?"

He seemed to consider this. "I guess I would."

"I hid it in the bus. I just didn't think the other girls should read it. Not that I'm trying to be mean. But I'm a writer and I keep a journal, and some things, well, they're supposed to be private, you know?"

He nodded. "And I'm hoping you will keep some parts of my story private too, Emily. I don't mind if you tell your friends that Dan was my son. And you can even tell them

about how stupid I was. But some things about Dan ...
well, some things are best left alone."

She nodded. "Don't worry. Your story is safe with me."

"And your family's story is safe with me too."

"So does this make us friends now?" asked Emily as
they headed down the dunes trail that led back toward the
trailer court.

"I reckon it does."

Emily paused where the trail forked over to the bus.
"How about if I get that journal while we're here?"

"I'd like that."

"You want to see the bus?" she asked, waiting and hoping that he'd follow her down the trail. "We've really fixed
it up."

So while she got the journal, he took a quick peek
inside, but then just as quickly he went back outside. "It
sure looks different in there," he said as she came out to
rejoin him.

"Kind of girly, huh?"

He grinned. "Yep, I reckon it is. But it does look nice."

Then she gave him the journal as well as the high school
yearbook. "Oh, yeah," she said. "Do you have a record
player?"

He nodded.

"Let me get something else for you, okay?" And she
hurried back in to get the Elton John album. "Listen to the

song called 'Daniel' on this record," she told him. "I think you'll like it."

He nodded and started to go, but then he stopped. "And since you feel like Dan was your friend too, well, you'd be welcome to come see some of his photos and other things if you'd like. Your friends can come too. I have them all set up in a room. Just to look at. I thought I'd gotten all of his stuff from the bus." He looked at the items in his hand. "Guess I missed some. Thank you for taking the time, Emily."

"*Thank you*, Mr. Greeley."

chapter ten

"Thanks for letting me come with you today," Emily said as she rode with Morgan's grandma to the airport. It was Saturday afternoon and Morgan and her mom's flight should've landed by now.

"We're supposed to get them by the baggage pickup," said Grandma as she turned toward the terminal. "You keep your eyes peeled and I'll drive as slowly as possible."

"No problem there," said Emily when she noticed the traffic jam up ahead. Grandma slowly made her way forward and Emily scanned the crowd for Morgan and her mom. "There they are!" she shouted. "Up there by the big turning door."

Soon they had Morgan and her mom and their stuff all loaded in the car and were heading out. "Thanks for the ride, Mom," said Cleo. "But I thought Leslie was getting us."

"She had to keep shop for you," said Grandma, "since Kara was sick today."

"I'm so glad you came!" said Morgan as she gave Emily's hand a squeeze. "I missed you so much. So tell me, have you been bored out of your gourd?"

"Not exactly," said Emily with a smile. "Although I'll admit that it has been pretty quiet."

"Have you seen Carlie at all?"

"A couple of times ... but she's been pretty busy with Miguel and Pedro. They're a handful. But I did help her take them to the beach yesterday. The weather finally warmed up again, and we played in the sand and stuff."

"I'm so happy to be home," said Morgan. "I mean, it was actually pretty fun in Atlanta. And I can't wait to show you guys some of the awesome stuff I got for free at the gift show — things we can use for the bus. Very cool."

"I'm so glad you're home too," admitted Emily. Then she lowered her voice, "and I do have something *big* to tell you when we're all together, back in our clubhouse again."

"Can't you tell me now?" begged Morgan. "It sounds really interesting."

Emily shook her head. "Remember what you said about being part of a club, Morgan. We need to consider the other girls too." Then she held up her hand with the bracelet and grinned. "Rainbows rule."

Morgan nodded and held hers up too. "Rainbows rule."

By the time they made it home from Portland, it was too late to have a club meeting, but Morgan said she'd call the girls for a two o'clock meeting tomorrow, after they got back from church.

"Sure you don't want to give me a hint about your big news?" asked Morgan as they dropped Emily at her house.

"It's a mystery," said Emily.

"Thanks a lot," said Morgan. But she was smiling.

"Glad you're home," said Emily again. "See you tomorrow."

The next day, on their way home from church, Morgan tried to pry more information from Emily, but Emily told her she'd have to wait.

"You're pretty good at keeping a secret," said Morgan as they pulled into the mobile-home court.

Emily nodded with lips pressed firmly together. Morgan had no idea!

Finally it was two o'clock and all four girls were back together in the Rainbow Bus. Emily put on a record to play, and they sat down at the table where Morgan set out a plate of her grandma's homemade oatmeal raisin cookies and a carton of milk. She'd also brought along a box full of things from the gift show for the bus. She had colorful notepads and magnetic pens and scented candles and bright silk flowers and stuffed gadgets and window decorations and all sorts of things.

"You should've seen the place," said Morgan. "It was huge, like acres and acres of these little shops with all this stuff. My feet got so tired."

"But was it fun?" asked Amy.

"Sure. And then they give you all this free stuff."

"It's like Christmas," said Carlie, holding up a stained-glass butterfly with a little hanger on it.

"For the bus," added Morgan. "Which reminds me, I did get some Christmas decorations too, but we can save those for later."

"It's so good to be back in the bus," said Amy. "And it's fun having music. That's a great place for the record player."

"So, how was music camp?" asked Emily, wanting to save her news for last.

Amy gave a complete rundown on music camp and who was there and how Amy got to do a flute solo at the campfire one night. "It was really pretty good," she said finally. "And it didn't seem that geeky."

"See," said Morgan. "We told you."

"And I made a hundred dollars this week," said Carlie proudly.

"Just for babysitting?" asked Amy.

"Just for?" repeated Carlie with wide eyes. "Do you have any idea how much work it is to take care of two little kids that never stop moving? And Pedro is barely potty trained. You know what that means?"

Amy laughed. "No. But it doesn't sound good."

"Well, that was a hard-earned hundred-dollars," said Carlie. "And then my parents made me put half into the bank for my college fund. And the rest … Mom says I should save to buy school clothes." She shook her head. "I think they're the ones who came out on top in that deal."

The bus got quiet now, and Morgan looked at Emily. "Emily has something to tell us," she said. "Something big."

Now all eyes were on Emily. Thankfully, she'd carefully rehearsed what she was going to tell them — and how much. She wanted to be respectful of Mr. Greeley, but she wanted them to understand the story too. Especially since they all got to share in the bus together.

"Well, I was putting away the books and I started wondering about Dan Watterson again."

"Oh, yeah, Dan the man," said Amy. "We almost forgot about that dude."

"That's right," said Morgan. "Don't tell me you figured it out?"

Emily nodded. "And it wasn't easy." She told them about some of her early dead ends and then how she finally remembered the old librarian. But she didn't mention the journal. She wanted that to remain private.

"Mrs. Drimmel?" said Amy. "Of course, she's been here forever."

"And she's so old, she'd know everybody," said Morgan. "Good work, Em."

"She was Dan's teacher in high school," said Emily. "And she totally remembered him. She said he was a nice kid. But she also said that shortly after college he went to Desert Storm."

"Desert Storm?" said Carlie. "What's that?"

"A war," said Emily.

"The Iraq War?" asked Amy.

"No, that's what I thought too. Desert Storm started in 1991, and Dan went in that year."

"He would've been about twenty-eight by then," said Amy.

"Thirty," corrected Emily, and everyone looked stunned. "I guess he had a late birthday," she added quickly. "Anyway, Dan Watterson was killed in action."

"Really?" Morgan looked stunned.

"That's sad," said Carlie.

"War is so wrong," said Amy in an angry voice.

"So he never made it back," continued Emily. "And this was his bus. He'd been touring the country in it ... after college. And he was kind of lost and confused ... He'd been in love with this girl from high school, and she sort of just disappeared on him. It was like he never got over her."

"Man, that's so sad," said Morgan.

"Was that why he went to the war?" asked Carlie.

"Maybe so ..."

"But why is his bus here?" asked Morgan.

"Well, that's the amazing part," said Emily. "Dan Watterson was Mr. Greeley's only son."

"But why wasn't his name Greeley?" asked Morgan.

"Mr. Greeley's wife left him when Dan was a little boy. She married another man who adopted Dan, and they changed his name. And poor Mr. Greeley didn't see Dan for years. He finally tracked them down in Boscoe Bay and moved here himself. That's when he started the mobile-home court. Dan was still in high school. He just wanted to be around him."

"That's sweet," said Morgan.

"Yeah. And they got to be friends and stuff."

"And then Dan went to the war and got killed?" said Carlie, her voice breaking as she said it.

Emily nodded. "Yeah. I was really torn up about it too. I felt like I'd really gotten to know Dan, like we were related or something."

"Well, we'll have to make sure that we honor his memory in our bus," said Morgan. "Maybe we can hang up a picture or something."

"That's a great idea," said Emily. "I'll talk to Mr. Greeley about it."

Morgan peered curiously at her. "So you're talking to Mr. Greeley now?"

Emily grinned. "Yeah. He's really nice. Just sad and lonely. But we're friends now. And he told me it was okay to tell you guys about Dan's story — since we're the owners of his bus."

"That's cool," said Morgan.

"So what kind of Christmas stuff did you get at the gift show?" asked Emily, quickly changing the subject.

"Huh?" said Morgan, caught off guard.

"Like, did you get any cool strings of lights?" asked Emily hopefully. "I was thinking that it'd be cool to hang some string lights in here. You know for those gray, foggy kinds of days, like the ones we had last week."

"That's a great idea," said Morgan. "And I did get a set of lights. They were actually the shapes of tropical fruit."

"That's perfect!" exclaimed Emily.

"You want to see them?"

"Yeah!" said Emily.

"Okay." Morgan was already pushing through the beads and going for the door. "I'll be back in five minutes."

As soon as Morgan was gone, Emily started talking. "Okay, you guys, it's Morgan's birthday on Tuesday, and I wanted to get her out of here so we could make a quick plan. All in favor of giving her a surprise birthday party say aye."

"Aye!" all three shouted.

"Okay." Emily grabbed the notebook. "Who's doing what?"

It was the quickest party-planning meeting Emily had ever been to, not that she'd been to many. But by the time Morgan came back, they had it all figured out. And to make their little act even more convincing, Emily got very excited over Morgan's tropical-fruit lights.

"Those are so great, Morgan!" she exclaimed as Morgan took them out of the box.

"They'll be perfect in here," said Amy.

"And I bet they don't use much electricity either," added Carlie.

"Good thinking to bring them in here, Em," said Morgan. "I'm really glad I didn't save them until Christmas."

"Well, I was in here a lot last week," said Emily. "And it was pretty gloomy outside. Seemed like we could use some more light."

Soon they had the lights suspended over the tiny dining table, and when Morgan plugged them in, everyone cheered.

"Look at all the colors," said Emily.

"Sort of like a rainbow," said Amy.

"Rainbows rule!" shouted Carlie, holding up her hand with the bracelet. And the other girls followed.

"It's good to be back together again," Morgan said with a big smile.

They spent the next couple of hours just hanging out, putting all Morgan's interesting goodies away, and listening to old vinyl records. And Emily thought it felt almost like coming home.

On Monday, Emily left the trailer park just a little before nine. She used the back exit so that Morgan wouldn't notice her from her kitchen window. Then she hurried toward town and finally turned into the Waterfront District where she knew Morgan's mom's shop was located. She'd seen Cleo's from the street, but up until now had never gone inside. But today she was on a mission.

"Oh, hi, Emily," said Cleo from where she was unpacking a box in the back of the store.

"Hi," said Emily, looking around the shop with interest, noticing all the colorful items from all over the world. There were pillows and dishes and statues and jewelry and clothing — all sorts of things. "This is a cool shop," she told Cleo as she walked toward the back.

"You've never been in here before?" asked Cleo as she unwrapped a large piece of pottery and set it on the counter.

"No, but I'll be sure to make it a regular stop from now on."

"So, what's up?" asked Cleo as she adjusted a brightly colored scarf that was tied loosely around her neck.

"I'm looking for something for Morgan's birthday," said Emily.

"That's so sweet of you," said Cleo.

"We're having a surprise party for her tomorrow — in the clubhouse — and I wanted to give her something special." Emily reached down to pat the small purse that was hanging over her shoulder. She still had most of her share of the people's choice winnings, but she'd need to save enough to buy birthday cake ingredients too. "Do you know of anything she's been wanting?"

Cleo rubbed her chin as she considered this. "Hmm..." Then she snapped her fingers. "I do!"

"What is it?"

"Come over here and I'll show you."

Emily hoped it wouldn't be too expensive as she followed Cleo over to where some wooden boxes were stacked. They looked really nice. Then Cleo picked up one of the larger ones and opened it. "Morgan's been wanting something just like this to keep her beadwork in."

"It's beautiful," said Emily, running her hand over the smooth surface of the wood. "How much does it cost?"

"Well," said Cleo, "how about if I give it to you at cost?"

Emily wasn't sure what that meant, but she nodded.

"That would be ten dollars."

"Really?" Emily couldn't believe it. How could a box this nice be that inexpensive? "Are you sure?" she asked. "I mean, I don't want you to —"

"I'm sure, Emily. You see, all my things are imported and I get some amazing buys. And, as I recall, cost on these boxes was really about ten dollars."

"Well, I'll take it," said Emily.

Cleo smiled. "Want me to wrap it for you?"

"Oh, yeah," said Emily. "I don't think we have any wrapping paper at home."

"Go ahead and look around the shop," said Cleo as she carried the box back to the counter.

Before long, the gift was wrapped and paid for and Emily was happily carrying the brown bag through town. She stopped by the little grocery store to get the cake things, including birthday candles, then headed on home.

"Watcha doing?" asked Morgan as Emily came into Harbor View with her bag.

"Just some shopping," said Emily, wishing she'd remembered to use the other entrance. "For my mom," she added, feeling a little guilty for the lie. But maybe it was okay under the circumstances.

The four girls got together to hang out in the afternoon, but no mention was made of the upcoming birthday, and Emily suspected that Morgan was feeling a little bummed that no one seemed to remember her big day. Then everyone, except Morgan, made up excuses to go home early. Emily knew it was so they could take care of their parts of the party preparations. Carlie was in charge of decorations, and she was going to make a mini-pinata. Amy was taking care of napkins and plates and things, promising that it would be really pretty.

"You guys coming over tomorrow?" asked Morgan as they went outside.

"I can't come over until one," said Carlie. "I have to babysit."

"And I promised to help at the restaurant tomorrow morning," said Amy.

"Why don't we just get together at one then?" suggested Emily, knowing full well that the three girls would be there sooner. And she'd already arranged with Morgan's grandma to sneak the bus key out and into the mailbox while Morgan was still asleep.

"Okay," said Morgan. But she looked disappointed.

"See ya tomorrow," called Emily as she left Morgan still standing by the abandoned bus.

The next day, Emily, Carlie, and Amy sneaked over to the bus at noon. Carlie had gotten the key out of the mailbox, and they let themselves in and quickly went to work setting up their surprise party. Shortly before one, the three girls stepped back to look at their accomplishment.

"The decorations are fantastic, Carlie," said Emily.

"Yes," agreed Amy. "So colorful. Morgan will love it."

"And the dishes and things you brought …," said Emily. "They're perfect too, Amy."

"That cake looks yummy," said Carlie.

"It's almost one," said Emily. "We should hide in the back of the bus."

"What if Morgan doesn't come?" asked Amy. "She might be worried about the lost key."

"I think she'll come," said Emily. "She'll have to explain to us why we can't get in the bus."

"But we won't be here," said Carlie. "If we're hiding."

"I'll leave the door open," said Emily. She ran up to open the door then back to where Amy and Carlie were waiting.

After about five minutes, they heard someone coming in the door. And sure enough it was Morgan. They all jumped out and yelled, "Surprise!"

"Whoa!" said Morgan, almost falling backwards out the door.

"Happy Birthday!" they yelled.

It was obvious that she was totally surprised, and this made the three girls even happier.

"You're a teenager now!" said Emily, giving Morgan a quick hug.

Morgan grinned. "And you guys aren't."

"I will be in November," said Emily.

"I won't be thirteen until next April," said Carlie.

"And I won't be thirteen for almost two years," admitted Amy. "How come you're so old anyway, Morgan?"

Morgan laughed. "My mom and I were living in Thailand when I was six, and she didn't start me in school."

"So you weren't held back?" said Amy.

"Amy!" said Emily in a scolding tone.

But Morgan just laughed even harder now. "No, Amy, I wasn't held back. I just didn't start first grade until I was seven. But I never really minded. I actually think it's pretty cool being older than everyone."

"I think it's cool that you got to live in Thailand," said Emily. "You'll have to tell us more about that."

"Not right now," said Morgan, eyeing the cake and presents.

And so Emily lit the thirteen rainbow-colored candles, they sang "Happy Birthday," and then Morgan blew them all out in one big breath.

"You'll get your wish!" exclaimed Emily.

"I already did," said Morgan, smiling at her three best friends. "It seems like my prayers and wishes just keep coming true."

Girls of Harbor View
by Melody Carlson!

Harbor view was no place for a girl ... until now. Meet Morgan, Amy, Carlie, and Emily, unlikely friends brought together when they come to live in the Harbor View Trailer Park. Discover what happens when they join forces to make their world a better place.

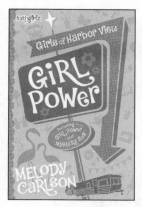

Girl Power

Take Charge

Raising Faith

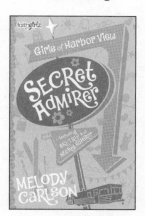

Secret Admirer

Available in stores and online!